The sound of a loud crash turned his blood cold. *Emma!*

The front door was wooden, old, with a flimsy dead bolt. Thunder boomed, and Reed took advantage. He rammed the door with a well-placed kick.

It shuddered and gave way.

He entered the house, his flashlight moving over everything. His breathing was ragged, but the hand holding his weapon was steady.

Which way? Upstairs or toward the back of the house?

He paused, straining to listen. There. A noise coming from the kitchen. He raced down the hallway. Someone was coughing.

His flashlight caught a dark figure bolting out the back door. Reed swung to his left. Emma sat on the tile floor, one hand holding her neck. Her face was red and her long hair stuck out in all directions. Relief replaced the terror in her expression when she caught sight of him.

D09963474

Lynn Shannon writes novels that combine intriguing mysteries with heartfelt romance. Raised in Texas, she believes pecans and Blue Bell ice cream are must-haves for every household. Lynn lives with her husband, two children, an extremely spoiled dog and a turtle who hibernates half the year. You can find her online at www.lynnshannon.com.

Books by Lynn Shannon

Love Inspired Suspense

Following the Evidence

FOLLOWING THE EVIDENCE

LYNN SHANNON

LOVE INSPIRED SUSPENSE
INSPIRATIONAL ROMANCE

If you purchased this book without a cover you should be aware that this book is stolen property. It was reported as "unsold and destroyed" to the publisher, and neither the author nor the publisher has received any payment for this "stripped book."

LOVE INSPIRED® SUSPENSE
INSPIRATIONAL ROMANCE

ISBN-13: 978-1-335-40294-3

Following the Evidence

Recycling programs for this product may not exist in your area.

Copyright © 2020 by Lynn Shannon Balabanos

All rights reserved. No part of this book may be used or reproduced in any manner whatsoever without written permission except in the case of brief quotations embodied in critical articles and reviews.

This is a work of fiction. Names, characters, places and incidents are either the product of the author's imagination or are used fictitiously. Any resemblance to actual persons, living or dead, businesses, companies, events or locales is entirely coincidental.

This edition published by arrangement with Harlequin Books S.A.

For questions and comments about the quality of this book, please contact us at CustomerService@Harlequin.com.

Love Inspired
22 Adelaide St. West, 40th Floor
Toronto, Ontario M5H 4E3, Canada
www.Harlequin.com

Printed in U.S.A.

For we walk by faith, not by sight.
–2 Corinthians 5:7

To my husband. I'm thankful to be walking through life with you by my side.

ONE

Emma jerked awake.

She automatically reached for the baby monitor on her nightstand. No cry or whimper came through the speaker, only the slight shushing sound of Lily's steady breathing. Her muscles relaxed. The baby was fine.

A bolt of lightning streaked across the sky, followed by a loud clap of thunder. The storm must have woken her.

Before Lily came along, there was nothing Emma couldn't sleep through. Now every creak of the house disturbed her, a side effect of motherhood. Of course, recent events also had her on edge. The threats...

Emma squeezed her eyes shut and forced the thoughts away. If she started pondering her new troubles, she'd never get back to sleep.

Texas storms could be fierce, and this one was no exception. Rain pounded against the roof. Wind whistled around the corner of the old house, a hollow, mourning sound.

A shiver raced down Emma's spine. She tried to snuggle back into her pillow but something felt off. Wrong somehow. She extended her leg, parting the covers near the foot of her bed. Warmth caressed her toes but no solid form interrupted her progress.

Where was Sadie?

A low growl came from the bedroom door.

Emma sat up. Her eyes hadn't quite adjusted to the dark, but she could make out the large blot of her dog near the doorway.

"What is it, girl?" Emma whispered.

Sadie didn't turn her head. Her body was rigid, the hair standing up on the back of her neck.

Fear, sharp and instinctive, coursed through Emma. The Labrador wouldn't behave that way if it was just Vivian, her sister-in-law, moving around.

Lightning momentarily lit up her bedroom and the corresponding hallway. No one was there.

Emma strained to listen beyond the sounds of the storm. It was impossible. The rain was coming down in curtains, the thunder as loud as a sonic boom. Sadie's ears twitched, and another warning growl rumbled through her chest. This one was sharper and more urgent.

Emma needed no further convincing. She threw off the covers and grabbed her cell phone. She hit the first number on Speed Dial.

A woman answered. "Heyworth Sheriff's Department."

"My name is Emma Pierce." She ran to her closet. "I live at 125 Old Hickory Lane. I think someone has broken into my home."

"Did you hear someone break in?"

Emma cocked the phone between her ear and her shoulder. Her hands shook as she pulled a small box from the top shelf. She ignored the dispatcher's question. It would be too complicated to explain Sadie had alerted her. "I need deputies sent to my home immediately. 125 Old Hickory Lane."

"I'm sending them now."

It brought Emma little relief. She lived in a rural area.

On a good day, she was twenty minutes from the sheriff's department. With the storm raging outside, it might take twice that long for deputies to arrive.

"Do you know who is breaking into your home?" the dispatcher asked.

"I can't talk right now," she said. "I'll call you back in a moment."

"Ma'am, stay—"

Emma hung up and fished a Taser out of the box. Her late husband had bought it as a security measure, an extra precaution when she left vet school late at night. She'd almost gotten rid of it when she moved to the countryside, but Mark's warning had stopped her.

You never know, sweetheart. You might need it.

She gripped the Taser with a shaking hand, simultaneously rising from her crouch and tucking her cell into the pocket of her pajama pants. Sadie followed her into the hall.

Emma had spent sleepless nights running this scenario through her mind. The threats from her cousin Owen were escalating.

When Uncle Jeb unexpectedly died and left Emma almost his entire estate, she'd been flabbergasted. Her mother's brother had been one of the last living blood relations she had. They'd talked on the phone regularly, had been as close as two people living on opposite sides of the country could be, but never did she imagine he would pass over his only child, Owen, and give her the lion's share portion of his estate.

It'd taken only one meeting at the lawyer's office to understand why Uncle Jeb hadn't left the property he loved so much to his son. Owen bounced from odd job to odd job, from girlfriend to girlfriend and spent most of his time with his hand around a liquor bottle. It would've taken him a few months to destroy what Jeb had spent a lifetime building.

Owen hadn't taken the news well. Her cousin had flown into a screaming rage at the lawyer's office. Shortly after Emma moved into Uncle Jeb's home, the hang-up phone calls began. Flowerbeds were destroyed and patio furniture broken. Minor annoyances became increasingly frightening when the phone calls took a more threatening tone and someone attempted to poison Sadie. After that, Emma reported it all to the sheriff's office. Her complaint hadn't been taken seriously.

Would Owen go so far as to break into her house in the middle of the night? She feared he might.

She entered Lily's room. The glow from the night-light glimmered off the little girl's hair and the curve of her cheek. Emma picked up her daughter, nestling the child's face against her shoulder. Lily stirred but, thankfully, remained sleeping. As silent as a shadow, Emma flew to her sister-in-law's room.

"Vivian," she hissed.

The other woman muttered something in her sleep. Emma placed Lily down gently on the bed before shaking Vivian awake. When her sister-in-law opened her eyes, Emma held a finger to her lips. "I think someone's in the house."

Vivian's eyes widened and her body went stiff.

"Take Lily into the bathroom and lock the door." Emma pressed her cell phone into Vivian's hand. "Speed Dial 1 is the sheriff's office. Deputies are on the way, but you should call them again."

Vivian grabbed her wrist. "Where are you going?"

"To check it out." Emma secretly hoped whatever had caused Sadie's reaction wasn't cause for serious alarm, but she wasn't taking any chances.

Vivian's gaze dropped to the Taser in Emma's hand. "Please…be careful."

Emma gave a sharp jerk of her head. "Bathroom."

Vivian flew into motion. Within moments, the bathroom door clicked closed. Before leaving Vivian's bedroom, Emma rested her hand against Sadie's head. The dog's fur was soft against her fingertips. Sadie glanced at her and Emma could almost hear the animal's thoughts. *Take me with you.*

"Stay," Emma whispered. "Guard."

If there was an intruder in the house and he managed to get past Emma, he would have to go through Sadie to hurt Lily or Vivian. The Labrador would fight to the death to protect her family—especially Lily. She'd been trained to.

Emma slipped out into the hall on silent footsteps. Her heart pounded against her rib cage. Possibilities played in her mind, the images flashing like her own personal scary movie. She was no innocent country girl—she knew full well the horrors people could inflict on one another. As a search-and-rescue volunteer, she'd seen it up close and personal.

Father, please help me be strong. Give me the ability to protect my family if necessary.

She paused at the top of the stairs. Her senses were on high alert. Warm, moist air washed over her and the rain seemed louder, like a door or window was open. She swallowed hard and gripped the Taser a bit tighter before edging her way down the staircase.

Bang!

She jumped and bit back a shriek. Her hands went numb. The wind screamed through the house, rattling the windowpanes.

Bang. Bang.

Trembling, she took a deep breath and rounded the

banister. The sound was coming from the kitchen. She raced down the dark hall, her slippers silent against the wood floor. She paused at the entrance to the kitchen and peeked around the doorframe.

One of the large glass panes on her bay window was broken, the shards scattered across the tile floor. The wind screeched again, rocking a cabinet door forward before slamming it closed. Water from the rain mixed with the glass on the floor. Was that…?

She stepped forward and caught a glimpse of leaves on the floor. A tree branch.

Heady relief washed over her. No one had broken into the house. The storm's high winds had simply thrown a branch through the glass. She lowered the Taser. A streak of lightning lit up the kitchen, making it as bright as midday. Emma saw them a fraction too late.

Muddy boot prints.

Something moved out of the corner of her eye. Emma spun. The Taser flew from her hand and a cookie jar on the counter shattered as the intruder tackled her.

The storm was a bad one.

Sheriff Reed Atkinson sat in his favorite chair on the screened-in porch and watched the rain batter against the barn. Wind whipped tree branches back and forth, the thunder so loud it vibrated in his chest. Lightning bolted from the sky, striking a nearby tree. Reed sucked in a breath as a limb cracked. It crashed to the ground, narrowly missing the barn's roof by inches.

Close. Too close. He made sure there weren't lingering sparks, but the rain drenched any fire before it could start. Reed settled back in his chair. He checked the time. A little after one in the morning.

He'd already called the sheriff's department and placed

himself on reserve. The standard units were working, but with a night like this, sometimes an extra hand or two became necessary. Everything was quiet when he spoke to his dispatch operator, Mona, and he hoped it stayed that way.

Still, he couldn't manage to sleep. Insomnia and Reed were old friends, albeit grudgingly.

The anniversary of Bonnie's disappearance was this month. His sister had been gone for a year, and there hadn't been a single phone call or email from her. Not even a letter. Her social security number hadn't been used, her bank accounts and credit cards remained untouched. Reed had been a cop long enough to know her case probably wasn't going to have the happy ending he wanted.

Yet, there was a niggle of hope he couldn't snuff out that she was alive. It's what kept him digging. It also kept him awake in the middle of the night.

Reed rose from the chair and stretched. Maybe he would try to lie down anyway. As he crossed the threshold into the tiny living room, his cell phone rang. The familiar number on his screen flashed and his heart skipped a beat. Dispatch.

He answered, his voice gruff but authoritative. "Atkinson."

"Sheriff, Emma Pierce contacted me a few minutes ago." Mona spoke in a rush. "She inherited Jeb Tillman's place."

"I know who she is."

A simple sentence that didn't begin to encompass the complicated relationship between Reed and Emma. They'd had a serious summer romance ten years ago before reality and different life goals sent them in opposite directions. Since Emma's move back to Heyworth last month,

Reed had done his best to avoid her. A ridiculous notion, considering the town's size. It was smarter to be polite.

Still, when he'd spotted her in the grocery store last week, the rush of emotion had caught him off guard. Reed had turned on his heel and walked the other way.

"She thinks an intruder has broken into her house," Mona said.

Reed's chest clenched. Emma was a widow with a small child. That made her an easier target for criminals looking to steal.

"I've dispatched the closest unit but with the storm, they're more than thirty minutes out," Mona continued. "Since you—"

"Got it."

Reed's ranch bordered Emma's. He could be at her house in less than five minutes—a huge, potentially life-saving time difference.

"How does she know someone is breaking in?" Reed shoved his feet into worn cowboy boots.

"She didn't say. I tried to keep her on the phone, but she hung up, claiming someone would call me right back."

"Contact the unit and let them know I'll be on site," Reed ordered. He didn't want to be accidentally shot by one of his own men.

"Will do."

He hung up and pulled on his holster along with his jacket. Within moments, he was sliding into the seat of his pickup truck and flying down his driveway.

Possibilities raced through his mind. Violent crime was almost nonexistent in their county, home invasions extremely rare. In this storm, she could have heard the wind rattling the house or had a tree branch shatter a window. Both of those would've sounded as though an individual was breaking in. An honest mistake. It'd happened before.

But what if it wasn't a mistake? It was always the question Reed asked himself whenever he rushed to a potential scene. He treated every case with absolute seriousness. Reed knew, better than most, even small towns like Heyworth had their darker elements.

God, please help me get there in time. Let her and her family be okay.

It'd been a long time since they'd dated, but if Emma was anything like the woman he used to know, she would be first in line to protect her loved ones. Reed battled against the images of her hurt or worse...

No. That wouldn't happen.

His headlights sliced through the darkness. The old country road was unpaved, narrow and rarely used. It was also the shortest route between his ranch and Emma's property. His tires ate up the gravel and it pinged against the undercarriage. He was going dangerously fast, but he couldn't slow down. If something happened to Emma or her family, he would never forgive himself.

Out of nowhere, another truck appeared, racing toward Reed. The vehicle had no headlights on, bouncing down the road at a reckless speed. Teenagers? His office had had a problem with racing on these back roads, but since Reed had become sheriff nine months ago, he'd cracked down on it.

A sick feeling twisted his stomach. Or could this be Emma's intruder? The truck was coming from the direction of her property. Reed tried to make out the make and model of the vehicle, but in the rain and the dark, it was impossible. He honked his horn, but the truck didn't change paths. It barreled down on him.

A blinding light filled Reed's windshield, obscuring his vision. The driver had turned on his brights.

Reed jerked his wheel to avoid colliding with the other

truck. His tires hit a slick spot and fishtailed. His heart jumped into his throat. He tapped his brakes, managing to bring his truck back under control before it skidded off the road and into the woods.

In his rearview mirror, the other vehicle disappeared. The driver hadn't even slowed down.

Shaken and angry, Reed allowed himself half a breath. Under normal circumstances, he would do a U-turn and arrest whoever was driving, but he didn't have the time for that now. He had to get to Emma.

He raced the rest of the way there. Before making the turn to her ranch, he killed his lights. If the intruder was still inside the house, Reed didn't want to alert him that law enforcement had arrived. That was a good way to turn a home invasion into a hostage situation.

Rain instantly soaked the shoulders of his jacket. In his haste to leave, Reed hadn't taken his hat. His hair became plastered to his head, water running in rivers down his face and into his collar. The grass was slick under his boots. Mud splashed the cuffs of his jeans as he ran to the front porch.

He scanned the front door and the closest windows with his flashlight. Nothing. Everything looked locked and secure. Lightning streaked across the sky, and above his head wind chimes danced. He needed to go around the perimeter of the house, look for signs of a break-in. The back door maybe—

The sound of a loud crash turned his blood cold. *Emma!*

The front door was wooden, old, with a flimsy deadbolt. Thunder boomed, and Reed took advantage. He rammed the door with a well-placed kick. His heel screamed in protest, but the wood splintered.

"Come on, come on…" He focused his energy on the

weak spot he'd created. He slammed into the door again. It shuddered and gave way.

He entered the house, his flashlight moving over everything. A banister leading upstairs. A dining room to his right. A living room to his left. His breathing was ragged, but the hand holding his weapon was steady.

Which way? Upstairs or toward the back of the house?

He paused, straining to listen. There. A noise coming from the kitchen. He raced down the hallway. Someone was coughing.

His flashlight caught a dark figure bolting out the back door. Reed swung to his left. Emma sat on the tile floor, one hand holding her neck. Her face was red and her long hair stuck out in all directions. Relief replaced the terror in her expression when she caught sight of him.

Reed bent down, scanning quickly for blood. How seriously had she been hurt?

"Go," she choked out. "I'm okay, and he's getting away."

Reed dashed after the intruder.

TWO

Reed's boots slipped on the mud and the grass as he rounded the corner of the house. Rain pelted him, and he blinked to clear his vision. The intruder was already across the yard, headed for the safety of the woods.

"Police!" Reed shouted. "Freeze!"

The dark form paid him no heed. Reed raised his gun, but the man was a quickly moving target. Reed had no shot. Within the span of two heartbeats, the intruder disappeared into the woods.

Reed wrestled with the need to give chase, but the rain and the dark put him at a distinct disadvantage. It wasn't smart to go into the woods without backup. Smothering his frustration, he pulled out his phone and hit Speed Dial while jogging back to the house.

Mona answered before the first ring finished.

"I need every available unit to my location. I also need an ambulance." He barked out his orders and a brief description of the suspect. Not that it was much. Male, roughly six feet, wearing dark-colored clothing and a ski mask.

He hung up and entered the kitchen.

Emma had turned on the lights, bringing the attack's destruction into full focus. A tree branch had obviously been used to break the window. It lay discarded. A shattered cookie jar was partly on the counter, the rest on the floor. A Taser resting on the tile sent a fresh wave of adrenaline through him. Had Emma been attacked with it?

She was standing with her back to him, one slender hand clutching the wall as if it was the only thing keeping her standing. Her breathing was raspy. There was no blood on the floor or on her clothes, but it didn't necessarily mean she was okay. Shock could be covering the pain.

Glass crunched under his boots. She turned at the sound of his approach. Her face was ashen, her eyes huge.

"It's okay. You're okay," he reassured her. He scanned her body for wounds, stopping at the sight of the red marks around her neck. His jaw tightened in anger. "Did he use the Taser on you?"

"No." Her voice came out barely above a whisper. "Just his hands. The Taser's mine, but he knocked it away before I could use it."

Other than the marks on her neck, Emma was remarkably whole. A few minor cuts from the glass on her arms. Her pajama top and bottoms were wet from the rain. Her whole body trembled. Whether from cold, fear or shock, he couldn't tell.

"The ambulance is on its way." Reed took off his coat. The outside leather was wet, but it was layered and would help warm her until the ambulance arrived. He draped it over her shoulders.

"Is he gone?" she asked.

"Yes." He pulled a kitchen chair around and gently led her to it. "Where's your daughter?"

"Lily is with my sister-in-law, Vivian. They're upstairs."

"Wait here."

Reed tore down the hall and ran up the stairs. A rumbling growl drew him up short.

A dog was standing in a doorway, teeth bared and hackles up. There was no doubt the animal would attack him if he went closer.

The stairs creaked as Emma came up behind him. "Stop," she rasped. The dog immediately ceased growling but remained at attention. "Good dog, Sadie."

"Can I move past her or is she going to bite me?" Reed asked.

"Sadie will only attack on my command now."

He took her word for it. The bedroom was empty, but he could hear the sounds of a baby crying on the other side of a door. Reed rapped on the wood. "It's Sheriff Reed Atkinson. Can you unlock the door, please?"

The lock clicked. A blond woman emerged, cradling a red-faced child. The vise around Reed's chest loosened, and he took his first deep breath. Vivian and the baby appeared unharmed and although Emma was hurt, her injuries were minor. Things could've been so much worse.

Thank you, Lord.

Vivian spotted Emma standing in the doorway and rushed around Reed.

"Thank God, you're all right." Vivian started crying. "I was so scared. When I heard the banging—"

"We're okay." Emma wrapped her arms around Vivian. "We're all okay."

Sadie joined the group, standing as close to their legs as possible. Emma took the baby, shushing her. Lily was gorgeous, with her mother's dark hair and eyes. Her chubby arms were wrapped around a stuffed lamb. Seeing Emma holding her little girl twisted something in Reed's gut.

"What happened?" Vivian swiped at her tears before tilting Emma's head to get a look at her neck. "You're hurt!"

"I'm okay. Reed stopped him before…" Emma's voice

trailed off and her grip tightened on the baby. "Unfortunately, he got away."

"He won't be free for long," Reed interjected. "Whoever did this will be caught, I promise."

Emma spun toward him, her eyes widening. "Really? So it took him breaking in and attacking me before you decided to stop ignoring the situation?"

Sadie, sensitive to her owner's temperament, growled, and Reed eyed the dog with trepidation. He held up his hands in a sign of surrender. "I know you're upset—"

"I'm not upset. I'm furious." Her cheeks flushed. "Tonight could've been completely avoided if you'd taken the threats I reported seriously."

Reed stiffened as her words registered. His gaze snapped to hers. "Threats? What threats?"

"This is your last warning. Heyworth is not your home. Leave or you will be hurt."

The voice coming from Emma's cell phone sounded mechanical and distorted. It'd been half an hour since the attack, and she'd changed out of her wet pajamas, but chills still raced through her. She clasped her hands together to keep her fingers from trembling.

"The phone calls started shortly after I moved here. They weren't all like that one. In the beginning it was just hang-ups, sometimes heavy breathing. I brushed them off, but then things started happening on the property."

A muscle in Reed's jaw worked, and his shoulders were tight. He looked furious but when he spoke, his voice was calm. "What kinds of things?"

"Equipment was moved, flowerbeds destroyed. A couple of my patio chairs were broken. Small stuff. Annoying but not necessarily threatening."

He scrawled something in a small notebook.

Reed's chestnut-colored hair was darkened from the rain but still carried the faintest impression of a hat indention. A dusting of stubble hid the cleft in his chin.

She'd often thought of Reed over the years, but it'd been a surprise to discover he was the sheriff. Reed always talked about the day he'd leave Heyworth in his rearview mirror. It was one of the many things they'd fought over—her desire to return to the small town, his eagerness to never see it again.

"You didn't report the phone calls or the things happening on the property?" he asked.

She bit her lip. "Not at first. It sounds foolish, I know, but I thought my cousin was doing it. Owen was dealing with a lot. First the death of his father, then the shock of learning about the inheritance."

"You felt bad for him." Reed's expression was sympathetic and nonjudgmental. "You were trying to give him the benefit of the doubt."

The understanding in his expression eased the guilt and shame pressing down on her shoulders. "Yes. I figured if I ignored him, Owen would eventually tire of it and stop. But last week, things took a more serious turn. Someone left poisoned hamburger meat near the back patio."

"Why would Owen do that?"

"I think he was trying to kill Sadie."

At the sound of her name, the dog raised her head. Emma reached down and stroked her silky fur.

"He obviously didn't know Sadie has been trained not to eat food from anyone except me and Vivian. Unfortunately, an opossum found the untouched meat and died. That's how I knew it'd been poisoned."

Reed frowned, his glance flickering to the dog before settling back on Emma. "You trained Sadie to only take food from certain people?"

"It's a safety measure. She's a SAR dog." Short for Search and Rescue, Sadie was part of an elite class of canines trained to find missing people. "But that's not the reason why I filed a police report. Even if Sadie wasn't specially trained, she's my pet and my responsibility. Attempting to hurt her was crossing a line and not something I could ignore."

He nodded. "How many people know about Sadie's training?"

"It's not a secret." She smiled wryly. "Still not dialed into the town gossip, huh?"

"Not unless it pertains to a case." His mouth flattened. "I didn't know about Sadie, but your uncle told me about your husband. I'm very sorry, Emma."

"Thank you." A rush of unexpected tears caught her off guard. Emma blinked them back. Mark had been dead for almost two years, and still grief had a way of smacking her in the face. "While we're getting personal, Jeb also told me about your mom. And Bonnie."

Reed's mother had passed away from cancer. Shortly after that, his sister disappeared. The events had to be connected to his return home, but it didn't seem right to pry into his reasoning.

"Thank you." He cleared his throat before the corners of his mouth lifted. "Your uncle was a man of few words, but he had a way of sharing the most important ones."

"That he did." She paused, a sinking feeling settling in the pit of her stomach. "I was told by the desk clerk that you review every complaint but…you didn't know, did you?"

"No. If I had, something would've been done about it." Reed's words resonated with conviction.

She bit her lip. He'd saved her life, probably Lily's and

Vivian's, too, and she'd thanked him with accusations and anger. "I'm so sorry—"

Reed held up a hand, cutting her off. "No, I'm the one who owes the apology. You were right to be angry. It's my job to protect you, and it didn't happen." He let out a breath. "I'm very grateful that you—that everyone—is okay."

Their eyes met. His were still the color of faded blue jeans. A flood of memories washed over her—church picnics, horseback rides and long talks by the lake. Emma felt a poignant stab at the loss of their friendship. But it hadn't escaped her notice that Reed had been avoiding her since she moved back to town. He'd nearly tripped over a paper towel rack in the grocery store trying to get away from her last week.

His behavior was the reason she believed her initial complaint against Owen had gone uninvestigated. She'd been mistaken about that. But while she'd misjudged him as a sheriff, Emma wasn't wrong when it came to their relationship. It was obvious Reed didn't want to be friends. The knowledge hurt. She didn't want it to, but it did all the same.

"The latest threatening message…" he gestured to her cell phone still on the table between them "…when did you get it?"

"Sunday, the same day I filed the police report. I thought the bad thing he referred to in the message was the poisoned hamburger meat." She glanced toward the kitchen. "Clearly, I was wrong."

He frowned. "I'm not so sure you were. Come with me."

Reed led her into the living room. Sadie's nails tapped against the wooden floor as she trailed behind Emma.

The living room had been ransacked. Drawers hung open, books were thrown from the shelves and knickknacks were knocked over. The little desk in the corner she used as an office had been torn apart. Paper littered the carpet.

She took a step farther inside, her legs trembling.

"Can you tell if anything is missing?" Reed asked.

She glanced around the room. "Without cleaning up, I can't be sure, but I do know my iPad is missing. It was sitting right there on my desk when I went to bed."

"And when you came downstairs, you didn't enter this room?"

"No, I went straight to the kitchen via the hallway."

She led him back to the banister and retraced her steps. Inside the kitchen, a deputy was dusting the doorknob for prints while another took photographs. Emma's gaze drifted over the broken bay window, the glass littering her kitchen floor and the shattered cookie jar. A coldness crept up her spine, stealing the breath from her lungs.

"Emma?" Reed stepped into her line of sight, dipping his head to catch her eyes. "We can stop for a minute if you need to."

"No. I'm fine." Emma realized she was absently rubbing her throat. She forced her hand down. "The attacker must have heard you or saw your flashlight, because he jumped off me and ran for the back door."

"Were you able to get a good look at him? Can you describe what he looks like?"

"No. It was dark, and he was wearing a ski mask. I didn't see anything." She scooted a leaf away with the edge of her tennis shoe. "I thought the branch had broken the window."

"He threw it inside to gain entry to the house." Reed glanced over his shoulder. "Then he went into the living room and started searching for stuff to steal. The noise from the thunderstorm would've covered his tracks."

"Except Sadie heard him moving around," she concluded.

"Yes. He probably saw you go right past the living room doorway to the kitchen. It spooked him, and he attacked."

"So you think it was a robbery then? Not something personal?"

His mouth tightened. "I don't know. I've got men out looking for Owen as we speak, but I don't want to jump to any conclusions. The threats could be connected to the break-in, or they could be two separate incidents. I'll know more once we're further into the investigation."

Vivian appeared in the doorway. She was dressed in jeans and a simple T-shirt, her hair piled on her head in a messy bun. On her hip, Lily bounced, stretching her arms toward her mother.

"She's tired, but I think she wants Mama," Vivian explained.

Emma took her daughter into her arms. She breathed in Lily's sweet smell, the familiar weight of her thirteen-month-old baby a reminder of her obligations and blessings.

Thank you, Lord, for protecting my family and for sending Reed in time.

The prayer soothed her, but it couldn't erase the dread as she surveyed the destruction in the kitchen. Could this have been a simple break-in gone terribly wrong? Or had Owen finally decided to take his opportunity to get rid of her once and for all?

THREE

Heyworth Sheriff's Department was a small red-bricked building tucked between the courthouse and a park. Midafternoon sunlight sparkled off the glass windows. Reed pulled into the parking lot and killed the engine. The scent of french fries from the diner across the street tickled his nose. His stomach growled. It was well past lunchtime and he hadn't eaten, but there wasn't time right now.

"Hey, Sheriff." Cathy, his daytime receptionist/dispatcher, handed him a stack of messages. "How's Owen?"

"Still in the hospital." It'd only taken an hour for Reed's deputies to locate Owen Tillman in the parking lot of a local bar. However, Owen was so inebriated, he had to be rushed to the hospital. Alcohol poisoning had nearly killed him. It had taken hours before Reed could question Emma's cousin about the break-in. "Is Deputy Shadwick here yet?"

She wrinkled her nose. "Waiting at his desk."

Reed went through the swinging half door separating the lobby from the rest of the department. "Shadwick," he called out. "My office. Now."

Reed ignored the attention from the others in the bull pen, his entire focus on the man marching to his office. Bald with a chubby face covered in a thick beard, Dean

Shadwick was dressed in a vest covered with fishing lures and wading boots. His mouth was tight and his body vibrated with tension, like an angry hornet, but he did his best to plaster on a look of veiled concern.

"I'm not in uniform because Cathy told me to come right in," Dean said, once they were both inside Reed's office. His eyes narrowed. "I was fishing on the lake when she called."

"I'll get right to the point." Reed circled around the broad expanse of his desk and set the stack of messages down. He purposefully didn't sit. "Did Emma Pierce file a complaint with you last Sunday?"

"Is that why you called me in?" Dean took his time settling into the visitor's chair. He stretched out his legs and crossed his arms over his paunch. "She did come into the station. I listened to her story."

Reed clamped down on his rising temper. He'd inherited most of his deputies when he took over as sheriff nine months ago. Dean was one of them. "And?"

"The phone calls seemed like a prank to me. A couple of weird things happened on the property, but they could be explained a hundred different ways." Dean waved a hand as if flicking away an annoying pest. "She was making wild accusations. Mentioned someone might be involved in poisoning her dog. Ridiculous."

"Deputy, I can't help but wonder if this report disappeared because Emma mentioned her cousin Owen as a possible suspect. I've seen the two of you around town, and I know you go hunting together."

"That has nothing to do with it." Dean glared at him. "I made a judgment call—"

"Which wasn't yours to make. It was mine."

The idea that someone's complaint had gone uninvestigated and a person had almost *died* as a result pushed every one of Reed's hot buttons, as a lawman and a human being. He knew firsthand what lackadaisical police work could do to a case. If the former sheriff had taken Bonnie's disappearance more seriously in the beginning, Reed's sister might not still be missing. He wouldn't allow another case in Heyworth to fall through the cracks. Not on his watch.

"Due to your incompetence, Emma was attacked last night in her home and nearly killed."

"What?" Dean paled. He swallowed hard. "Is she… I mean, is she all right?"

His deputy's shock and concern seemed genuine, which tampered Reed's anger a touch. "Thankfully, no one was seriously hurt. This time. But if you'd filed the report and we had investigated properly, the attack on Emma might've been prevented. You are suspended, Deputy, without pay for two months. After that, you will be on probation for the next year. Desk duty with an overseeing deputy watching over you."

Dean shot to his feet. "That's insane!"

"Count your blessings. I could fire you."

Dean's mouth popped open as if he was going to say something, but Reed's glare stopped him. The deputy's lips flattened into a hard line and his nostrils flared.

"Let this be a lesson to you." Reed softened his tone. "Don't let your personal feelings cloud your professional duty."

"You can't seriously think Owen had anything to do with the attack on Emma." Heat tinged the tips of Dean's ears bright red. "He's got a temper but he isn't stupid."

"It doesn't matter what I think. If Owen was innocent, an investigation would've proven it. You messed up, Deputy, by trying to protect your friend. You're dismissed."

Dean left his office with the flurry of a five-year-old in

the midst of a temper tantrum. Reed watched through the blinds of his office window as Dean stormed out. Reed felt no guilt at the punishment he'd doled out, but neither did he take pleasure in it.

Austin Carter, his cousin and chief deputy, appeared in the doorway. His dark hair was cut military short. A faint scar, etched out by an errant bicycle handle when he was eight, marred his upper right cheek. "Hey, Emma's here. She came into the department while you were talking to Deputy Shadwick."

Reed's brow furrowed. "Is she okay?"

"Fine, but she wants to talk to you. She's waiting in the break room. I didn't think it would be a good idea for her and Dean to cross paths, all things considered."

"Thanks." Reed hesitated. "Did you tell her anything about Owen being in the hospital? Or the developments in the case?"

"No. I figured it would be easier coming from you."

Reed walked quickly down the hall. Emma was standing next to the window in the break room. She turned at the sound of his approach, her lips tipped up in a smile. Sunlight caressed the elegant curves of her face and brought out the red highlights in her dark hair. She was dressed simply, in jeans and a T-shirt, but it only made her beauty that much more striking. Reed's breath hitched.

"Hi," she said. "Sorry to barge in on you like this, but I cleaned up the mess from the break-in and discovered something else was stolen."

"Of course." His gaze dropped to her neck. Bruises marred the delicate skin, and his gut clenched. Emma was special, a piece of his childhood and his first love. But he needed to keep his emotions in check and his head in the game. Otherwise, he might make a mistake on the case. "What is it?"

She reached into her purse and pulled out a photograph. Her hands were slender, the tips of her fingers long and the nails unpainted. "Uncle Jeb's gold pen was taken. It's not extremely valuable, although I'm sure you could sell it to a pawn shop for several hundred dollars." She handed him the photograph. "He used it to sign the deed to the original property. This is a picture taken on that day. Sorry, I don't have a close up of the actual pen."

"That's okay. Was anything else taken besides the iPad and pen?"

"No, that's it. Were you able to find Owen and talk to him?"

"Yes." He hesitated. The last thing he wanted to do was worry Emma, but he had to tell her the truth. "There's a strong possibility Owen isn't behind the attack, Emma. The perpetrator might be someone else."

Emma blindly reached out and grabbed the back of a chair as the implication of Reed's words slammed into her with the force of a freight train. "Are you sure?"

"Owen has an alibi for last night. The bartender at the Silver Spur said your cousin was there from six o'clock in the evening until closing time."

Her mind raced. As frightening as it was to have Owen stalking her, it was exponentially worse to have a stranger doing it. "My house is only five miles from the bar. Could Owen have slipped out without the bartender knowing?"

"I considered that, but the amount of alcohol Owen drank last night would make it nearly impossible for him to have the coordination and wherewithal to break in to your house." Reed took a deep breath. "My deputies discovered Owen in the parking lot of the Silver Spur this morning suffering from alcohol poisoning. He had to be rushed to the hospital."

She pulled the chair out and sank into it. "Is he okay?"

"Thankfully, yes. The doctor said there was a strong possibility he could've died if we hadn't been out looking for him and gotten him to the hospital in time."

Emma closed her eyes as a rush of pain radiated through her chest. Her relationship with Owen hadn't always been so rocky. They'd been close as children. "I'll contact my uncle's attorney and have him pay Owen a visit. I didn't get all of the inheritance. Uncle Jeb set up a trust for Owen. He'll receive it if he goes to rehab and remains sober for a year."

Maybe this time her cousin would take the help. She feared if he didn't, Owen's addiction would kill him.

Reed pulled out the chair across from her and sat down. "Did you know Jeb was going to name you in his will?"

"No, although he must've been thinking about it for a long time. We often talked about my hopes and dreams for the future, especially after Mark was killed in combat. It was in my plans to move to Heyworth before Lily started school, but I wanted to save up money to open Helping Paws first."

His brow furrowed. "Helping Paws? What's that?"

"It's the nonprofit organization I'm starting. Search-and-rescue dogs have been a passion of mine since vet school. I adopted Sadie five years ago and got my certification to be a trainer. It was always my dream to start a SAR canine-training facility. The goal is to train and provide SAR dogs to law enforcement and fire departments at no charge."

"That's amazing. The nearest SAR dog we have is more than three hours away. I haven't been able to convince the county to set aside the funds to purchase one."

"You aren't alone. There's a serious shortage of SAR dogs and most law enforcement departments in rural communities don't have the money to purchase them. Which is frustrating. Dogs like Sadie save lives. That's why I'm so passionate about this project. But a facility like the one I want to create takes a significant amount of income to get off the ground. You need the buildings and all of that, but the biggest expense is the land."

"You need a large area to do the training."

She nodded. "Uncle Jeb wrote me a personal letter, which he gave to the probate attorney. In it, he encouraged me to use his ranch to build Helping Paws."

She was deeply saddened by Uncle Jeb's death, but the opportunity he'd provided wasn't something she could pass up. It would've taken far longer to get her organization started without the inheritance.

Reed drummed his fingers on the table. "Can you think of anyone who might want to hurt you?"

"No." She bit her lip. "Everyone in Heyworth has been so welcoming, and other than Owen, I haven't had any altercations with anyone."

She got up from the table and went over to the window. In the park nearby, she spotted Vivian pushing Lily in the baby swing. Her daughter's chubby hands clung to the seat, and she kicked her legs in joy.

"What am I going to do, Reed? I have a child to protect and a criminal stalking me." She crossed her arms over her chest, hugging herself. "Vivian packed up her life to follow me to Heyworth, to help me raise Lily and get Helping Paws off the ground. I've already sunk most of my savings into making improvements on Uncle Jeb's land and getting the necessary equipment. God put this mission in my heart, and I want to see it through."

"And you will."

She turned. Reed came up close. His chin jutted out and his shoulders were squared. Emma knew that look. She'd seen it many times before, usually at the beginning of an argument. Reed was stubborn as a mule when he set his mind to something.

"I'm going to get to the bottom of this," he continued. "In the meantime, a deputy will be watching your property day and night. My top priority is keeping you and your family safe."

Some of the tightness left her chest. She took a deep breath. "Thank you, Reed. I can't tell you how much better it makes me feel to have you working on this."

"I'm glad. I want you to know you're safe. Heyworth is your home." He reached out and touched her arm. "This is where you belong."

Warmth spread though her. Emma's childhood had been spent bouncing from place to place behind a mother who flitted through life like a hummingbird. She'd gone through thirty schools, dozens of friends and a handful of stepfathers. Coming to stay with Uncle Jeb the summer before her first year in college had been like a breath of fresh air. She'd fallen in love with Heyworth. The townsfolk all called each other by name, brought casseroles when a baby was born or a relative died, and told the same stories dozens of times.

Emma had vowed a long time ago to set her roots down in this town. There were only a handful of people who knew about her dream to live here. Reed was one of them. That he remembered touched her deeply.

It also set off alarm bells. Reed had made it clear he didn't want to be friends. The break-in had forced an interaction, but there was still an awkwardness to it, as if neither of them could navigate the new waters they found themselves in. She wasn't quite sure how to address it.

Will Norton stepped into the break room. Tall and handsome, with blond hair and the physique of a quarterback, Will was the golden boy of Heyworth. His uncle was a judge and he'd followed the family tradition by becoming the county's prosecutor.

Will paused midstep and his gaze flickered from Emma to Reed and back again. "Oh, uh, sorry to interrupt. Austin told me you guys were back here."

Emma's cheeks heated as she suddenly became aware of how closely she and Reed were standing to each other. She jumped back. "No, you aren't interrupting anything. How are you, Will?"

"Fine. Although I think I should be asking you that question. I heard about the break-in at your place. Are you okay?"

"Yes. Thanks to Reed, no one was hurt."

"I heard. Nice job, Sheriff." Will ran a hand down his silk tie. He looked like he'd just come from court, dressed in a crisply pressed shirt and slacks. "Do you have any suspects?"

"We're taking a hard look at Owen, but he has an alibi." Reed gave a quick version of the information he'd uncovered during his investigation. "Emma's been receiving threats, and I suspect the break-in is connected to those."

"Hmm…" Will rocked back on his heels. "Did you consider any of the people who wanted to buy Jeb's property?"

Reed's eyebrows shot up. "You had offers to buy the land, Emma?"

"I did, but I never considered them seriously." She frowned. "You think someone might be trying to scare me into selling?"

"It's a possibility. Who made offers?"

"My uncle did," Will said. "That's what made me think of it."

Emma nodded. "There was only one other person. It

was my other neighbor, the one on the south side. What's his name? Joshua something or other."

Reed stiffened. "Joshua Lowe."

"Yeah. That's it. Why, do you know him?"

Reed shared a look with Will. "You could say that."

FOUR

Reed knew Joshua Lowe well, but not because they were friends. Joshua was a small-time criminal and the town bad boy. He'd claimed to have changed his ways and was trying to be a respectable rancher, but reputations were hard to shake.

Joshua had also been secretly dating Bonnie at the time of her disappearance. Almost no one had known about the relationship, including Reed. That Bonnie kept it a secret wasn't surprising, considering Joshua's notoriety. But it hurt Reed all the same when he'd learned about it while retracing Bonnie's last steps on the night of her disappearance.

Bonnie and Joshua had made a plan to run away together. They were supposed to meet at a local park. Joshua claimed when he arrived, Bonnie wasn't there. He tried calling her, but she didn't answer.

Reed didn't believe him. Joshua refused to answer any questions about where he was in the hours prior to or directly after driving to the park. That fact, coupled with his criminal history, made Joshua the prime suspect in Bonnie's disappearance.

Given their history, it wasn't wise for Reed to interview Joshua by himself. He arranged for one of his best deputies to meet him on the ranch. Deputy Kyle Hendricks climbed out of his patrol car with a grunt.

"How ya doing, Sheriff?"

"Fine." Reed shook Kyle's hand. "Thanks for coming."

They located Joshua in the barn. He'd backed a dented farm truck up to the double doors and was loading hay bales into the bed. The thirty-year-old looked nothing like an all-American rancher. His long hair was pulled back into a man bun and tattoos covered his arms from shoulder to wrist.

"Joshua," Kyle called out as they approached.

Joshua turned and lifted a hand to block out the sun. His gaze settled on Kyle first, before jumping to Reed. Something flickered in the depths of his dark eyes but disappeared behind a shuttered expression of indifference.

He resumed loading his hay, tossing it with ease. "Deputy Hendricks. Sheriff. What can I do for you?"

Out of habit, Reed glanced in the cab of the truck. It was worn—the passenger seat ripped and the stereo missing—but there was no obvious contraband or drugs. "We need to talk with you about a recent attack."

Joshua stilled. "What kind of attack?"

"I'm surprised you haven't heard."

"I don't listen to gossip, Sheriff. I've been on the wrong end of it one too many times to pay it any mind."

There was a kernel of truth to the statement. Joshua had brought on his own troubles, but many of his exploits had been exaggerated by the townsfolk. Some were flat-out false. Reed suspected that if Joshua's mother wasn't still living in town, he would've left Heyworth a long time ago. "Emma Pierce's home was broken into, and she was nearly killed."

Joshua met Reed's gaze. "And you think I had something to do with it?"

"Did you?"

Joshua's jaw tightened. "No." He threw another hay bale into the truck with more force than necessary. "Why would I?"

"You put in an offer to buy her property after Jeb died, son." Kyle plucked a piece of hay out of the nearest bale and placed it in between his teeth. "A sizeable one. I spoke to Emma's attorney. He said you upped it to nearly double what the land is worth. And since Emma moved in, she's been having trouble with a stalker."

Joshua snorted. "So what? You think I got mad she wouldn't sell to me, so I decided to terrorize her into it? And when that didn't work, I broke into her home and tried to kill her?"

"Your interest in the property gives you motive. Where were you last night?"

"Home." Joshua raised a gloved hand. "And before you ask, no one can confirm it. I was by myself." He leaned against the truck and muttered something about never being left alone, before taking a deep breath. "Yes, I did offer to purchase Jeb's property after he died. I'm trying to expand my cattle-rearing operation and I need land to do it. Judge Norton has already told me many times that he isn't willing to sell any more of his property."

The Norton family had sold Joshua a piece of their land, but he was boxed in on three sides by the rest of their ranch. His only other neighbor was Emma to the south.

"However, when Emma turned me down," Joshua continued, "I made inquiries into buying the property Old Man Franklin has for sale."

Reed's gaze narrowed. "When did you do that?"

"Last week."

That was convenient. Joshua was smart and this wasn't his first run-in with the law. Reed wasn't going to let him off the hook so easily. "If you were willing to buy another piece of land, then why offer so much for Emma's?"

"Because having the property next to mine would've been far better. Since Emma refused to sell, I didn't have many other options available. Old Man Franklin's land is three miles away, which makes it a nuisance, but the price is right."

"Has your offer been accepted?"

"We're still negotiating, but I figure things will be settled by the end of next week. I have absolutely no motive for wanting to run Emma off her land, nor would I ever hurt her."

Reed scoffed. "You'll have to excuse us if we don't take your word for it."

Joshua's cheeks, already flushed with exertion, darkened to a deep red. "I'm many things, Sheriff, but I'm not a liar."

"We both know that's a load of baloney. You refused to answer all of my questions about Bonnie's disappearance."

"Which is my right, under the law. That doesn't make me a liar. I've already told you everything I know. Bonnie and I were supposed to meet that night. I was running late. When I got to the park, she was gone." Joshua fished a set of keys from his pocket. "If you'll excuse me, I have cattle to feed."

He marched toward the driver's side of the truck but paused with his hand on the door. Without turning around, he said loud enough for Reed to hear, "No matter what you think, I loved Bonnie."

Joshua climbed into the old truck and the engine sputtered to life. Dust flew out behind the vehicle as he sped across the pasture.

Reed watched him go, uncertainty settling into his gut

like a bad meal. "We need to follow up with Old Man Franklin."

"Agreed." Kyle unearthed a handkerchief and mopped his brow. "I'll stop by there on my way back to headquarters, although if what Joshua's saying checks out, he doesn't have a motive for wanting Emma off her land."

"Or he could be smart enough to make an offer on Franklin's property to make it *look* like he doesn't have a motive. Let's check with Old Man Franklin and take it from there."

Kyle and Reed walked back to their vehicles. Kyle drove off, but Reed slowed his SUV and pulled over to the side of the road. He took a deep breath to calm his rattled nerves. Joshua's words echoed in his mind.

I loved Bonnie.

Loved. Past tense. As if Joshua somehow knew she was dead.

Reed squeezed his eyes shut. He wouldn't go down that path until it was a certainty. Joshua's word choice cast doubt on his innocence, but that was nothing new.

As if of its own volition, Reed's hand reached for the cell phone hanging from his belt. He flipped through the messages to the right one and hit Play. His sister's voice came from the speaker.

"Hey, Reed. I was hoping you would be able to answer. You're probably working a big case or planning a stakeout or something. My big brother, the crime fighter. Listen, I really need to talk to you about something important. Can you call me back ASAP? It's urgent. Thanks. Love you."

Bonnie's tone was resigned, as if she'd somehow known he wouldn't return her call for hours. It reverberated inside him, mingling with the guilt and the frustration, until he wanted to exit his vehicle and punch a tree. Instead, he took a deep breath. Then another. His gaze drifted to the rearview mirror and the reflection of the ranch behind him.

Joshua had a motive for wanting Emma gone. Trying to scare her off the property so she would sell wasn't a far-fetched proposition. Still, Reed couldn't let his emotions get the better of him. Bonnie's case was separate from Emma's, and right now, Emma's had priority.

Two days after the break-in, Emma was trying to settle back into a normal routine. The attack and the threats kept crowding into her mind. True to his word, Reed had kept a deputy stationed at her house. There hadn't been any threatening phone calls and nothing on the ranch had been disturbed, which should have eased her worries but only put her on edge. She couldn't shake the feeling something bad was going to happen.

Emma threw a tennis ball and Sadie, nothing more than a flash of golden fur, streaked across the grass. She caught the ball midair. Her doggie grin was evident even across the distance separating them. They'd just finished a search-and-rescue training session. Another night of thunderstorms had left the ground muddy and Sadie would need a bath now, but Emma was grateful for the distraction.

Sadie dropped the ball at her feet. Emma picked it up. "One last throw and then it's bath time for you. Vivian and Lily are going to be back from the grocery store soon."

The dog pranced in anticipation. Emma hurled the ball and Sadie took off. The wind shifted, rustling the hair on the nape of Emma's neck. A creepy sensation of being watched flooded her.

She turned and peered into the trees, but nothing moved. She shook her head. Her imagination was running away with her.

"Ms. Pierce?"

Emma screamed and jumped, whirling around.

Deputy Jack Irving stood nearby. He lifted his hands. "Hey, hey. Are you okay?"

She closed her eyes, putting a hand on her chest. Her heart thundered against her palm. "I didn't hear you coming. Sorry for screaming. I've been a bit jumpy the last couple of days."

"After everything that's been going on, I don't blame you." He offered her a sympathetic smile. "I came out to tell you it's shift change now. Deputy Miller is taking over. He'll do a perimeter check first, so you won't see his car for a while. I didn't want you to worry."

"Thank you. That's very kind. Have a good night, Deputy."

He tipped his hat to her. "You, too, ma'am."

She watched him drive off and checked her watch. Reed should be arriving soon. He'd called earlier and asked if he could come by to give her an update on the case.

Sadie rolled around on the grass. Her paws, caked with dried mud, wriggled in the air. Emma chuckled. "Okay, you. Fun time's over."

She hooked a leash to Sadie's collar and brought her over to the hose. The dog's steps dragged as she realized what was about to happen. Emma dropped a kiss between her eyes. "It'll be quick. I promise." She tied Sadie to the porch post. "Stay right here and I'll run inside to grab the shampoo."

She retrieved it in a flash, pausing to make sure the new front door was closed securely behind her.

Sadie barked.

Emma spun and her heart stuttered.

Owen was standing on the bottom porch step. His face was mottled with rage, his eyes narrowed to tiny slits.

"What exactly do you think you're doing, going to the sheriff and accusin' me of things?"

She took a step back, but there was nowhere to go. Owen had her trapped. She glanced around desperately but didn't see Deputy Miller's vehicle. He was probably still doing a perimeter check. Emma broke out into a sweat and the taste of her own fear, sharp and metallic, filled her mouth.

"I didn't say—"

"Liar!" Owen slammed his hand against the railing.

On the other side of the porch, Sadie went crazy. She barked, straining against the leash.

"You told them I was sending you threatening messages, that I tried to attack you."

Swallowing past the terror clogging her throat, Emma tried to keep her voice calm and authoritative. "I told the sheriff you were angry with me over the inheritance. I didn't lie or accuse you of anything."

He came up the porch steps. Emma squeezed her hand around her house keys. They cut into her palm. Yes! She wasn't completely defenseless.

"This house, this land…" Owen gestured widely "…it's mine. It belongs to me."

She maneuvered a key in between her fingers. A makeshift weapon. Not great, but it could still do some damage. "How did you get past the deputy, Owen?"

He blinked, caught off guard by her question. "I cut through the woods."

The woods? The same place she'd felt someone watching her. It was also the same place the intruder had run to the other night. Owen had an alibi for the break-in, but that didn't clear him of the phone calls or the destruction around the property. Could more than one person be involved? A cold trickle of sweat dripped down her back.

"It's time for you to go, Owen. I don't want you here."

"You don't get to decide that."

He stepped closer. The scent of whiskey poured off his skin like a bad cologne. Emma fought the urge to gag.

"You're the thief here." He jabbed a finger at her. "You're the fraud. I'm not going to let you take what should be mine!"

He was so close she could see the individual threads of red in his bloodshot eyes. His breath was hot and rancid.

Emma tightened her grip on her keys. She didn't want to hurt him, but she would if she had to.

Jutting her chin, she looked him in the eye. "I said you need to go."

FIVE

Reed heard the barking first. It was insistent and alarming, growing louder as he took the turn into Emma's drive. Sadie was tied to the side of the porch. She strained against her leash. Reed quickly ascertained the dog's problem.

Owen.

The man had Emma cornered and was screaming in her face. The sight made Reed's blood run hot.

He radioed for the deputy patrolling Emma's property and slammed on his brakes. As he shoved the truck into Park, Sadie broke free of her collar. The dog bounded onto the porch and with a flying leap, tackled Owen. He let out a scream as Sadie's jaws clamped down on his arm and he stumbled backward down the stairs. Sadie didn't let go. The dog dragged Owen to the ground.

Reed raced across the yard, pulling out his handcuffs. "Call her off, Emma."

She gave a command, and Sadie immediately released Owen. Tears ran down the man's face as he cursed up a storm. Reed flipped him over and slapped the cuffs on him. "Owen Tillman, you are under arrest for trespassing, criminal threatening, public intoxication and anything else I can think to throw at you."

"What are you doing?" Owen screamed. "Her dog attacked me, and you're arresting me. I need to go to a hospital. Call an ambulance."

Emma appeared with a first aid kit in her hands. Reed shook his head. "We'll get the EMTs to do it. You don't have to."

"It'll take time for them to arrive. He's hurt. It might be his fault, but I'm not going to let him go untreated. He's bleeding pretty badly."

Owen glared at Emma. "Don't you dare touch me, you—"

Reed added some pressure to Owen's hurt arm and he cut off in a yelp.

A patrol car raced up the driveway. Deputy Miller clambered out. "I was on the far side of the ranch checking out the old barn for any recent activity. I'm so sorry."

"It's not your fault," Emma said, quickly reassuring him. "You can't be everywhere at once."

Reed hauled Owen to his feet. "Take this man to the hospital for treatment of his arm and to get him sobered up."

Owen screamed and cursed the entire way to the patrol car. The glare he shot Emma from the back of the vehicle iced Reed's blood. It also made him question everything he knew about this case.

Emma sat on the porch steps. The wind rustled her hair, blowing some strands across her forehead. Her face was pale and her body trembled. She stroked Sadie, who was tucked up next to her side.

"Are you okay?" Reed asked. "Did he hurt you?"

"No, he just scared me." She smiled weakly. "We have got to stop meeting like this."

"I couldn't agree more." He picked up the first aid kit from the step and fished out a cold pack. He activated it. "Put your head down to your knees."

She waved him off with a shaky hand. "I'm fine—"

"You're crashing from the adrenaline, Em." The old term of endearment slipped out of his mouth before he could catch it. He pushed Emma's head gently toward her knees and parted the silky strands of her hair, placing the cold pack on the back of her neck. "You pass out on the porch steps, and Vivian will read me the riot act for sure."

Sadie licked Reed's arm. He patted her on the head. "And you are such a good girl. What a hero. I'm buying you a box of doggie treats." He sat on the porch step on the other side of Emma. "Where is Vivian? And Lily?"

"They went to the grocery store. I messaged them while I was inside getting the first aid kit to make sure they were okay." She sucked in a deep breath, then another, before lowering the ice pack from her neck. "I feel better now. I don't know why that shook me so much."

"Owen is family. It's far more personal."

She nodded, twisting the ice pack in her hands. "Reed, Owen told me he cut through the woods to get onto the property. It's the same place the intruder escaped on the night I was attacked. Do you think it's possible Owen is working with someone?"

"It's something to consider. Owen doesn't hang out with a law-abiding crowd, and while he doesn't have the cash to hire someone to break into your house, your iPad and Uncle Jeb's pen may have been payment enough." His jaw tightened. "This little stunt he pulled gives me enough probable cause to get a search warrant for his phone records. I'm also going to question his friends again. If Owen did arrange for someone to break into your home, I'll find out."

He wasn't going to take Joshua off the suspect list either. Owen's attack just now was reckless and impulsive. It was in line with his personality and fit with a pattern of addiction. However, the stalking and break-in had been planned and well orchestrated. Reed wasn't sure Owen had the patience or discipline to pull off the criminal acts.

"How did your interview with Joshua go yesterday?" Emma asked, cutting into his thoughts.

"Joshua admitted he wanted to purchase the property, but when you refused to sell, he made an offer on another piece of land. Deputy Hendricks spoke to the other buyer—Old Man Franklin—and confirmed it."

"Well, that's a relief." Emma rose from the step and smiled down at Sadie. "You might be a hero, sweetie, but you're also still muddy."

"You aren't going to give this poor dog a bath after all her hard work."

"Afraid so." Her mouth twitched. "Wanna help?"

"Oh, no. She and I are working on becoming friends. I'm not about to mess that up by dousing her in soap and water. Besides, I have my own work to do."

Her brow crinkled. "You do?"

"I noticed you don't have floodlights on your house, so I went to the hardware store and picked some up."

Reed opened the rear of his SUV and pulled out a couple sacks from the local hardware store. He set them on the grass. "It's a bit presumptuous of me and I hope you don't mind, but the lights will make it easier for the deputies to see the yard."

"I don't mind at all. I appreciate you thinking of it." She smiled at him before patting Sadie on the head. "Come on, girl. Bath time for you." She started to turn away.

"Uh, wait." Reed reached out to stop her, his fingertips brushing along the soft skin of her arm. He jerked his hand back. Emma frowned, a flash of hurt crossing her pretty features.

Lord, I could really use some help here.

He didn't want to act on his attraction to Emma, but he didn't want an underlying tension between them either. Problem was, Reed wasn't great at dealing with the emotional baggage in his life. His sister had always been the one to steer him in the right direction. It was times like these he missed Bonnie's advice more than ever.

"Listen, Emma, I know things are a bit awkward between us and I don't want them to be." He shoved his hands in his pockets. "We're going to run into each other, not just in town, but also professionally. It's only a matter of time before we need you and Sadie to aid in a search. I hope... well, I hope we can be friends."

"Reed, you saved my life. I'm pretty sure that places you on the friend list permanently."

"Oh." The knot in his stomach loosened. "Good, cuz I could really use another set of hands to help me hang these lights."

She laughed. "Well, then you're going to have to help me bathe Sadie."

"Sorry, pup. She wrestled me into it." Sadie barked twice, and Reed nodded. "Right you are. Two boxes of cookies."

Emma laughed again. This time, Reed joined in, some of the weight pressing on his shoulders dropping away. He'd tackled one problem.

Now, he just needed to figure out who was stalking Emma and why.

Lily banged her tiny fists on her high chair tray and babbled.

"Hold on, little one." Emma snagged a slice of cornbread and broke it into pieces over the tray. Lily promptly fisted the crumbs and shoved them into her mouth. In the corner, Sadie snored on her bed.

Vivian handed Emma a set of plates for the table and some cutlery. "So what are you going to do about Owen?"

"Reed's going to continue his investigation, but he also recommends I take out a restraining order. Although Owen's been arrested for his actions today, it doesn't prevent him from making bail or being released from jail later. It's clear I have to do something."

"I'm glad he's taking these threats against you seriously."

"Me, too." Emma frowned. "You gave me one plate too many."

"No, I didn't. I invited Reed to dinner while you were giving Lily her bath." Vivian wiped her hands on her apron. "He ran home to clean up, but he should be here any minute."

Emma recognized the gleam in her sister-in-law's eyes. Heat crept into her cheeks. "Don't start matchmaking, Vivi."

"I have no idea what you're talking about. I merely invited the sheriff to dinner. It's the polite thing to do, considering he saved our lives." Vivian turned on the stove and picked up a spoon to stir the gravy. "But since you brought it up, I did recognize his name. He's *the* Reed. Your first love."

"That was a long time ago. A lot has changed since then."

"So what? A little romance never hurt anyone."

"Been there, Vivi, done that. And I have the broken heart to prove it."

"I know you do." Vivian sighed. "But Mark wouldn't want you to pine for him for the rest of your life. He's been gone two years. You've mourned him longer than you were married."

It was true. They'd dated, gotten engaged and were

married all within eight months. Emma often wondered if the loss was more poignant because of the short time she'd had with Mark. She'd been robbed of lazy Sunday afternoons, the chance to see him go gray at the temples, the deepening of their blooming love into something as endless as the ocean. It all died with Mark, leaving her pregnant, with a chest of empty dreams.

Vivian removed the gravy from the stovetop. "I think you could do a lot worse than a handsome lawman. I mean, think of the stories you'll tell your grandchildren. He literally rescued you like a knight in shining armor."

Emma rolled her eyes. "You've been watching too many movies. Reed and I are just friends."

"Downplay it all you want, but I've seen the way Reed looks at you. Mark my words there's something there."

A knock came from the front door and Vivi waggled her eyebrows. "That's for you."

Emma pointed a finger at her sister-in-law as she moved toward the living room. "Behave."

Sadie trailed behind her to the door, tail wagging. Emma swiped her hands on her jeans as a few butterflies fluttered in her stomach. "Don't be silly," she muttered to the dog. "It's just Reed. We spent hours with him this afternoon hanging the lights and talking about the case."

Reed turned on the stoop when she opened the door, his lips tipped up into a smile, and those traitorous butterflies took flight. He'd changed out of his uniform into a denim button-down shirt the same shade as his eyes. It molded over his broad shoulders. "Hey."

Her throat tightened painfully, but she managed to choke out a greeting. His boots thumped on the tile entryway and the scent of his soap, warm and piney, wafted in her direction.

Sadie barked. Reed patted her on the head. "No treats yet, girl. I didn't have time to go to the store."

He lifted a mysterious tinfoil-covered object in his other hand. "I brought my Aunt Bessie's apple pie. She makes extras for me and I keep them in the freezer. If we pop it in the oven now, it'll be ready in time for dessert."

"That's perfect."

Emma escorted him into the kitchen. She busied herself with turning on the oven and setting the pie inside while Reed greeted Vivian and Lily. The next few minutes were a rush of final preparations, pouring iced tea into the glasses and grabbing extra napkins. Then they all gathered around the table and Emma said grace.

"Everything looks delicious." Reed picked up his fork. "Thank you for the invitation."

"After all you've done, I think we owe you a couple of home-cooked meals," Vivian said with a smile. "Emma tells me you're from Heyworth. How long—"

Sadie barked. Then she growled, the hair on the back of her neck standing on end.

Reed shot out of the chair. His hand flew to the gun holstered at his waist. "Stay here." Within three strides, he was at the back door. "Lock this behind me."

He disappeared into the night. Emma flicked the lock before grabbing a knife from a block on the counter. She ushered Vivian and Lily into the large walk-in pantry, shutting the door behind them and planting herself in front of it.

"Stay," she ordered Sadie. "Guard."

The dog stood next to Emma. Moments ticked by, the tension building with every passing breath. Where was Reed? Was he okay? Emma whispered out a prayer for his safety.

Sadie's ears perked as a scraping sound came from the

back door. A shadowy figure appeared. The new motion detection spotlight they'd installed clicked on, but from this angle Emma couldn't see through the panes of glass in the door. She tightened her hold on the knife.

"Emma, it's me."

She let out a sigh of relief and hurried to unlock the back door for Reed.

"I checked around the house, but it's secure," he said. "None of the other motion detection lights went on." Reed's gaze dropped to Sadie. "Is it possible she was barking at an animal? I spotted some tracks that looked like opossums."

"It is. Sadie's well trained, but she's used to living in the city."

Then again, it could be more than that. Reed didn't say so, but he didn't have to. Emma instinctively understood that someone could've been out there, hidden in the woods just beyond the house.

The pantry door squeaked open and Vivian poked her head out. "Is it safe?"

"Yes." Emma took another breath to slow her racing heart. She set the knife down in the sink. "Turns out Sadie was probably scared of some opossums."

Vivian let out a bark of laughter. "Well...nothing like a little excitement to go with dinner."

Lily gave a screech of displeasure and leaned toward the table.

"Right, you are, Lily," Reed said. "I'm starving, too. Let's eat."

Emma didn't think she could stand to put a bite of food in her mouth. Her stomach was aching. But she joined them at the table anyway.

"Vivian, did Emma ever tell you about the time she attempted to make Uncle Jeb some eggs?" Reed's mouth curled up and he made a point to stare at the kitchen ceiling. "I'm certain they're still baked into the paint."

They all laughed, the tension easing. From there, dinner was a series of stories punctuated by Lily banging on her high chair for more food.

When they were all stuffed, Vivian rose from her chair and started to clear the table. Emma got up to help her, waving Reed back down into his seat. "It'll only take a few minutes. Rest."

Emma rinsed off the dishes and stuck them into the dishwasher before pulling the pie out of the oven. She carried it to the table, her footsteps faltering.

Reed had removed Lily from her high chair. Her head rested against Reed's chest and her tiny hand played with a button on his shirt. He was murmuring something to her, his deep voice soothing but too low to hear the actual words. Sadie lay at his feet.

Something inside Emma's chest twisted, perilously close to her heart. Lily had never known her father. Seeing the little girl cuddled up to Reed sent a wave of mixed emotions churning through Emma.

Vivian came up behind her, gently squeezing her arm, before taking the pie from her hands. "This is beautiful but looks too hot to eat at the moment." She set it on the table. "And Ms. Lily is looking tired. I'll take her to bed while we wait for the pie to cool." She lifted Lily from Reed's arms and bustled out of the room.

Emma backed toward the kitchen. "I'm gonna wash the pots while we wait."

"I'll help you by drying." Reed rose and joined her at the sink. He picked up a dish towel. "I noticed the construction you're doing on the north side of the property. Is that going to be the training facility?"

"Yep. I'll do the initial training with the dogs, but once

they're ready to be paired with a handler, there has to be additional training with them together. The handler will have to stay for a few weeks. I want to make that process as easy as possible, so I'm building small homes for them on the property."

"How far along are you?"

A strand of hair fell into her face. She pushed it back with her shoulder since her hands were covered in suds. "I'm about half done. Another month or so and we should be in operation." She scrubbed the pot and the hair fell in her face again. This time she attempted to blow it out of the way. "It helps that Uncle Jeb didn't clear huge swatches of the woods on the property. They'll be useful for the initial training. Once the dogs are more advanced, we'll use the nearby national park."

Reed's fingers skimmed the side of her face as he tucked the annoying strand behind her ear. Her breath hitched. "Thanks."

"Sure." He took the clean pot from her. "Will you breed the dogs yourself or buy them?"

"Actually, we're going to take dogs from the animal shelter. Most people aren't aware that SAR canines don't have to be purebreds. Sadie isn't." At the sound of her name, the dog raised her head. Emma smiled at her. "SAR dogs need specific traits like agility and a good nose. The pups that don't make it through the training program, we'll adopt out to loving homes. Vivian's good with accounting and fund-raising. She wants to handle the paperwork, which will free me up to do the training."

"It sounds amazing, Emma."

"It's a lot of work, but like I said before, God put this mission in my heart." She peeled off the kitchen gloves. She hated to ruin their easy conversation by bringing up a tough subject, but there would never be a great time to ask. "Reed, what happened to Bonnie?"

He let out a sigh, long and low. "She—"

Reed's phone trilled. He glanced at the screen and stiffened. "I have to take this. It's Dispatch."

He answered, walking to the other side of the kitchen. There were a few tense moments of silence. Emma sent up a prayer that whatever had happened God would watch over the innocent.

Reed hung up and turned to her. "I need you and Sadie to come with me. We've got a missing girl in Fairhill National Park."

SIX

In a missing person case, every second counted.

Reed's SUV bumped over the dirt road heading deeper into Fairhill National Park. Dusk was shifting into twilight and fireflies flickered in the trees on either side of the road. He ached to push down on the gas pedal, but the vehicle's suspension wouldn't survive.

"I've never been to this park," Emma said. She gripped the handle of the passenger seat as Reed swerved around a divot in the road. "Does this road lead to the main camping area?"

"No. Camping is allowed anywhere in the park, not just the designated areas. Molly—that's the missing girl—her dad is something of an outdoorsman. He likes to rough it."

She slanted a look his way. "You know the family?"

"Not well, but Derrick owns the hardware store in town. His wife is a teacher at the elementary school."

"How long has Molly been missing?"

Reed glanced at the clock, the knot in his stomach tightening. "About two hours. Derrick was smart to call us in early."

They rounded the bend and a campsite came into view with a family-size tent, fishing poles and a fire pit. One deputy was off to the side with two young children. Austin was near the tree line talking with Molly's parents. He broke off when he spotted Reed's vehicle.

Emma hopped out and opened the back seat to release Sadie from her specialized belt.

"We've got a missing eleven-year-old female, Molly Hanks." His chief deputy skipped the pleasantries and jumped straight into a report. "Last seen wearing black jeans, a gray T-shirt and purple sneakers. She disappeared while her parents were making dinner. They did a quick search of the nearby area and didn't find her. The park rangers were called in and they did a more extensive search but haven't located her yet."

"Where was she last seen?"

"She was reading over there." Austin gestured toward the far side of the clearing. A novel, split open to save the page, rested on a fallen tree trunk. "I've called in for assistance from the state troopers, as well as the Texas Rangers. The nearest SAR team has also been alerted, although they're a couple of hours away."

"Emma and Sadie are trained in Search and Rescue. They're going to give us a head start."

Austin tossed her a brief smile. "Good to see you again, Emma. Appreciate your help." He turned back to Reed. "This could be more than Molly simply wandering off and getting lost. We could be dealing with a possible abduction."

Reed shoulders stiffened. "How so?"

"Derrick isn't Molly's biological father. He's her stepdad. Apparently, the family has had issues with Molly's father in the past. He's a drug user and recently lost his visitation. According to the mom, he didn't handle it well."

"Got a description on Dad?"

"Name's Vernon Hanks. Last known address is in Willowbend." Austin pulled up a photograph on his phone—a copy of a driver's license photo. Vernon had a gaunt face with a handlebar mustache. "Molly and her father still communicate on the phone. She told him about this trip during their last conversation."

Reed's gaze jumped back to the book resting on the log. "Let's reach out to our counterparts in Willowbend, see if they can locate Mr. Hanks. I also want a BOLO out on any vehicle registered to him."

With a Be On The Lookout alert, every law enforcement officer in the state would be watching for the vehicle. If Vernon had managed to abduct his daughter, Reed didn't want him getting too far.

Reed reached into his trunk and pulled out a spare bulletproof vest. He handed it to Emma. "Put this on."

Her eyes widened slightly but she put it on before grabbing a backpack and slipping it over her shoulders. Sadie was already outfitted in a reflective vest. "I'm ready when you are."

Reed grabbed his own backpack with food, water and equipment. He had no intention of getting stuck out in the woods, but it was prudent to take precautions.

Another couple of squad cars drove up. Detective Kyle Hendricks got out.

"Hand over the scene to Hendricks. I want you with us," Reed said to Austin. "I've got enough supplies in my pack for two. Just grab an extra flashlight."

He spared a few more moments to speak to Molly's parents and explain what they were doing before joining Emma at the fallen log. "Do you need an article of clothing?"

"No. Sadie's an air-scenting dog. She'll find any person in the area."

Emma unhooked the dog's leash and gave a command. Sadie lifted her nose and headed into the woods. The bells attached to her vest jingled, making it easier to follow her, even in the dark.

Reed followed behind, urgency fueling him. Somewhere an owl hooted above them. Emma's ponytail bobbed with every step. She kept right on Sadie, increasing her stride as the dog went faster. Her brow was drawn down, her focus entirely on the mission at hand. Reed stayed next to her, close enough to reach out and touch her, even as he continuously scanned the trees and brush with his flashlight.

Austin called out for Molly, his voice carrying through the woods. The ground sloped upward in a steady incline. Reed's heart thumped with exertion and his feet slid slightly on the pine needles coating the forest floor. Sweat dripped down his back, causing his shirt to stick to his skin.

Sadie sped up, breaking into a run, and disappeared around a bend. She barked. Reed held Emma back with his hand.

"Stay behind me," he whispered. It was likely Molly was on her own, but he wouldn't take chances. Not with anyone, but especially not with Emma.

Austin palmed his weapon, and Reed did the same. They separated slightly, using the trees as cover. Emma followed closely behind Reed, matching him step for step as they made their way down the other side of the slope to the small valley below. Darkness surrounded them, making it impossible to see any danger lying around the next bend. Sadie's barking grew louder.

Reed's flashlight lit up a purple tennis shoe. Molly lay crumpled on the ground, tears streaking her face. Sadie stood next to her. He scanned the immediate area, but there wasn't anything suspicious.

"Molly, don't be alarmed." Reed smiled and bent down

next to the girl. "I'm Sherriff Atkinson. This is Lieutenant Carter and Mrs. Pierce." He pulled a bottle of water from his bag and unscrewed it. Molly took a long drink.

Austin pulled out his radio and attempted to call in.

Emma moved around to the other side of the girl. She praised and patted Sadie before slipping off her pack. "You're hurt. I have some first aid supplies in my pack. Can you tell me what happened?"

"I fell." Molly lifted a hand to her head. Her eyes were dazed, and she was shaking. "I rolled down the hill. My head... There's a lot of blood. And my ankle. I shouldn't have followed my dad out here."

Reed scanned the nearby trees. No movement. He yanked out an emergency blanket and opened it. "Where's your dad now?"

"I don't know. He left me here."

Emma placed gauze on Molly's head. "Reed, can you shine your flashlight over here for me so I can see better?"

The wound on Molly's head was huge. Reed wasn't a doctor, but he knew enough first aid to understand the child could be suffering from a concussion. In the background, Austin was still trying to get someone on the radio.

Reed scanned the trees again. Something about this didn't feel right. Why would Molly's dad go to all the effort to kidnap her only to leave her in the woods? His gaze fell on Sadie and then shifted to Emma. Unless...was it possible this was some kind of trap? To lure them out here?

Something whistled. Bark on the tree behind Austin exploded as the sound of a gunshot carried through the night. Austin dove for Molly as Reed threw himself over Emma. She yelled a command to Sadie. The dog bolted into the trees for cover as ordered.

Gunshots rained down, pelting the ground and the trees

nearby. Reed widened his body, cradling Emma's head against his chest to protect her. His heart thundered, even as his brain calculated their next move.

A bullet slammed into his back.

Emma's pulse pounded so loudly in her ear, she almost missed Reed's sharp intake of breath. Alarm ricocheted through her. Had he been shot? She tried to lift her head from his chest to ask, but he held her tighter. Emma could do nothing but pray he was okay.

The gunshots stopped; the sound of the last one seemed to echo through the night. Emma drew a ragged breath. Her body trembled.

"We need to move while he's reloading," Reed whispered in her ear. "There's a cave a short distance away. Follow Austin."

Before she could formulate a thought, Reed sprang to his feet, bringing her with him. Austin scooped up Molly and took off.

"Run!" Reed pushed her forward. Emma ran, doing her best to keep Austin's dark, shifting form in sight. Her feet pounded against the forest floor. Sadie appeared at Emma's side, keeping pace.

A gunshot rang out. Dirt sprayed, pebbles hitting against her jeans. She urged more power into her legs.

Lord, please, keep us safe.

The dark cave beckoned, and Emma flew into its embrace. Chest heaving, she turned in time to see Reed join them. He dropped her backpack on the cave floor. Sadie crowded next to Emma, seeking comfort. Reed and Austin both pulled their weapons.

"I want my daughter!" The voice carried across the forest. Molly's face paled, and she shook.

Emma put her arms around the girl. "Your dad?"

She nodded, tears streaming down her face. "I tried to tell him I couldn't go with him but he wouldn't listen. We had an argument, and he pushed me. I fell down the hill." Molly gripped Emma's arms. "Please don't let them shoot him. My dad does drugs and—"

"It's going to be okay." She couldn't do anything about the shooter outside, but she could comfort a frightened child. Molly was only eleven years old. Smart enough to understand the bad decisions her father had made, too young to emotionally cope with the consequences.

Reed and Austin were talking quickly. Making a plan, maybe? Austin again tried to radio in.

Emma moved Sadie next to Molly. "This is my dog. She's pretty scared, too. Hold on to her."

Molly dipped her hands into Sadie's soft fur and a sob rose in her throat. Emma fished out an emergency blanket from her backpack and tucked it around the young girl.

Reed looked at his phone and shook his head. He and Austin shared a tense few words. Emma joined them, keeping her voice hushed. "What is it?"

"Austin's radio was damaged, and mine isn't getting through," Reed said. "We also don't have reception on our cells. We can't call for help. Molly's dad was shooting from the ridge but he's on the move."

Reed winced as he lifted his arm attempting to get some reception. Emma grabbed his elbow. "Are you hurt?"

"He took a bullet to the vest," Austin said, without turning his head from where he was standing guard.

Emma's mouth went dry as irrational fear gripped her. She ran her hands along Reed's back. Her fingers brushed against the hole in his lightweight sheriff's jacket.

He grabbed her hand and squeezed it. "I'm fine and—"

"And we're sitting ducks," Austin said. "Give me your

radio. I'll head for higher ground to see if I can get some reception and call for help."

"I'll go."

"Not with your injury. The bulletproof vest saved your life, but we both know getting shot isn't painless." Austin put his hands on his hips. "You're going to move slower than I will due to the bruising on your back."

Reed's jaw tightened, but he nodded. "Be careful."

"Always." Austin slipped out of the cave and disappeared into the shadows. The dark would help him stay unseen. It could also make it easier for someone else to sneak up on him.

Emma bit her lip and sent up another prayer for his safety.

"We need to move," Reed said.

"Molly's hurt. And so are you."

"There isn't a choice." he whispered. "Vernon saw us go into the cave, and it's the first place he'll come looking. There's no way out of here. Austin and I used to hike up here as kids. There's another cave close by with an exit in the back. It'll give us an escape route."

Emma crouched down and fished the Taser out of her backpack. It wouldn't help much in a gunfight, but it was something.

"Molly, I'm going to carry you over my shoulders," Reed explained softly. "Please stay very quiet."

The little girl nodded, and he lifted her into a fireman's carry. His mouth hardened, the only indication the extra weight hurt his back. Holding Molly in that manner left his weapon hand free.

They eased into the dark forest. Cicadas sang. Sweat trailed down Emma's back as she strained to listen for anything out of the ordinary. A branch snapped. She froze.

Reed lifted a finger to his lips. The silence stretched out so long Emma wanted to scream from the weight of it.

Finally, Reed glanced at her and shook his head. He waved her forward. Together, they slipped into the next cave.

How long had Austin been gone? Ten minutes? If he wasn't able to get reception, how long would it be before Reed's men came looking for them? A thousand questions and possibilities rolled through Emma's mind as she arranged the blanket back over Molly. Sadie took her position next to the little girl.

Reed disappeared into the back of the cave and returned. "The exit is clear. Right down that pathway."

Gunfire erupted, breaking the stillness of the night. Austin shouted. There was the distinct sound of an object—or a person—crashing down the embankment.

Reed took a few steps forward toward the mouth of the cave. He stopped.

"Go," Emma whispered. She lifted the Taser. "I've got this and Sadie for protection. Go help Austin."

"No."

"You can't leave him out there by himself." Emma wouldn't forgive herself if they didn't try to help. She was almost certain Reed wouldn't either. "You've seen Sadie in action. You know she's capable of taking someone down. I'm not defenseless, but Austin might be. Go!"

He looked past her to the dog and Molly huddled together. "Get farther into the cave, hide in the shadows." Reed touched her cheek, his fingers as light as a butterfly wing. "Don't come out no matter what you hear."

Her throat tightened as the magnitude of his words sank into her skin with sharp claws. Only two hours ago, he'd been holding Lily. Now he was walking into a possible shoot-out with a criminal.

He turned and, on silent footsteps, slipped into the forest.

A breeze blew, whistling through the cave. Goose bumps rose on Emma's arms. A sense of foreboding washed over her. She'd prayed for Mark every day, but that hadn't prevented his plane from crashing in the middle of a war zone.

She gave herself a mental shake. There wasn't time to ruminate about her heartbreak. There wasn't anything she could do to help Reed beyond pray. Right now, her focus needed to be on keeping Molly safe and that started with moving the girl farther into the cave.

Using a flashlight wasn't an option. She didn't want to alert the shooter to their new hiding spot. Without it, however, she couldn't see well. Emma had a momentary fear of disturbing a bear or some other animal. That would be just the icing on the cake. But of course, Reed had gone in and come back out just fine.

"Molly, how are you doing?" Emma asked, keeping one eye on the cave's entrance as she bent down next to the girl. Sadie greeted her with a small lick to the shoulder. "How's your head?"

"It hurts."

The wound had stopped bleeding, but a large lump had formed next to her temple. Emma touched Molly's hands and found them ice-cold. Shock? She wouldn't be surprised. It only made their situation more dire. The need for medical attention was increasing with every minute.

"Let's move back a little." Emma helped the girl up and together they maneuvered farther into the shadows. Molly was already covered with one blanket, but Emma pulled out a second one. She wrapped Molly in it. "Keep your hands on Sadie. She's as good as a furnace."

The dog settled between them, her ears perked. Sadie

seemed to sense Emma's tension and unease. She was guarding without being told.

"I'm sorry. I didn't know my dad was going to shoot at you." Molly's voice was slightly slurred. It only ratcheted up Emma's anxiety.

"Don't worry, honey. This isn't your fault."

"No, it is. It is." She took a shuddering breath. "I told him I was mad at my mom… I shouldn't have… And he made a deal with someone. He said it was the only way we could be together…"

An icy chill raced down her spine. Emma bent down and held the girl's chin in her hand. Her eyes were nothing but deep shadows in her face. "Molly, is your dad out there with someone else?"

A twig snapped. Sadie stood, her body leaning forward.

Emma whirled. She peered through the darkness but saw nothing except shadows and shifting branches.

There. A flashlight moving through the forest.

Heading in their direction.

SEVEN

Reed moved through the forest like a shadow. Every step made his back ache, but he smothered the pain behind a wall of steel, along with the self doubt about his decision to leave Molly and Emma behind in the cave. He'd mitigated the danger by hiding them in a second location, but still, it was risky. The deciding factor hadn't been just about helping Austin—although that was huge—it was getting in contact with Dispatch. Reed couldn't protect them all on his own. He needed help.

Wind rustled the leaves. Reed paused, holding his breath. A sliver of moonlight slipped out from behind a cloud, catching on the edge of a black boot. His heart skittered. He lifted his weapon and edged closer.

The boot turned into a shape. The moonlight glinted off the barrel of a gun.

"Police. Don't take one more step."

Reed sucked in a breath and lowered his weapon. "Austin, it's me."

He stepped out of the shadows and his cousin's eyes widened. Austin was sprawled across the forest floor. Leaves and pine needles covered his clothes. Reed crouched down next to him. "Where are you hurt?"

"Forget about me." Austin gripped his arm. "Your instincts were right, Reed. Emma's the target. Molly was just an excuse to get her out here. Backup is on the way, but you need to get back to Emma. Hurry!"

Reed took off. His boots skidded against the pine needles and branches tugged at his clothes as he raced through the woods. The mouth of the cave came into view. Reed tightened his hold on his weapon and whispered Emma's name.

The cave was empty.

The muzzle of a gun touched the back of his head. Reed froze.

"Got ya." A pair of night vision goggles landed on the ground. "Okay, Sheriff, this is how it's going to be. Put your gun on the ground real slow and no one will get hurt."

Was it Molly's dad, Vernon? Had to be. Reed twisted his head, catching a glimpse of the handlebar mustache out of the corner of his eye.

"No one has gotten hurt so far, Vernon." Reed kept his voice even, no hint of his inner turmoil bleeding through. "Let's keep it that way. Why don't you put the gun down and we can talk?"

"We are way beyond talking, but I could be persuaded to let you live. Where is Emma?"

Thank you, Lord. Vernon didn't have her. "Why?"

"What do you care?" He applied more pressure to the rifle, the cold steel digging into Reed's skin. "You're going to put your gun down and you're going to show me where she's hiding. Along with my daughter."

Not a chance. "Okay, sure, Vernon. I'm going to put the gun down now."

"Yeah. Nice and slow."

Reed started lowering himself down to one knee. *One... two...*

He whirled up, grabbing the muzzle of the rifle.

Vernon stumbled. The gun went off, the sound like an explosion in the close confines of the cave. Reed kneed Vernon in the stomach and wrenched the weapon out of his hands.

A furry object flew past him and slammed right into Vernon. Sadie. Together the dog and criminal toppled over. Something whacked against the side of the cave, and Vernon yelped. Sadie held him trapped, snarling and barking.

Emma emerged from the rear of the cave. Breathing heavy, his back aching, Reed handed the rifle to her. He pulled out his handcuffs. "Call her off."

Once the dog backed away, Reed flipped Vernon around. He slapped the handcuffs on him and quickly read him his rights.

Outside, voices called out their names. Emma ran to the mouth of the cave, flipping on her flashlight and escorting the first responders to the rear of the cave. Probably where she'd hidden Molly. Reed patted Vernon down. He found a bag of drugs in his front pocket. "Why are you trying to kill Emma?"

Vernon glared at him. "I want a lawyer."

"I'm sure you do."

Reed picked up the cup of freshly brewed coffee from the vending machine. He took a long sip, letting the warmth and caffeine surge through him, before dropping in more coins for a second cup.

The hospital's emergency waiting room was mostly empty. Austin was still being examined by doctors. Emma sat in a plastic chair, talking on her cell phone. Her clothes were covered in mud and grass stains. Sadie sat at her feet, still wearing her SAR vest, allowed in the hospital because of her specialized training.

Reed's chest tightened. He didn't want to think about the number of ways tonight could've gone terribly wrong.

He took the second cup of coffee from the machine and crossed the room just as Emma hung up. He handed her the drink. "Everything okay with Vivian and Lily?"

"Yes." She sighed. "Vivian's more worried about me than herself. She says it's like a fort at the house. Deputy Irving is inside and there's another deputy on patrol around the property. Thank you, Reed, for arranging it."

"I told you, keeping you and your family safe is my first priority."

Not that he was doing a great job. Within the course of a couple of days, Emma had been threatened, choked and shot at.

Her hair had fallen loose from its ponytail. The strands curved around her face. A pine needle was tangled in them. Without a thought, Reed reached up and pulled it out. His fingers brushed across the silky threads of her hair.

Emma laughed lightly and took the pine needle from him. "I must look a fright."

"You look like someone who saved the day. Having Sadie take down Vernon probably saved my life."

It was a strange fact to acknowledge. Not that Emma had put herself on the line for him or Molly. That wasn't surprising given her character. But still, she was a civilian. Reed was used to relying on his men. Law enforcement was a brotherhood and there was an understanding each would give his life for another. Emma had no training in that regard, or any obligation. It made her bravery even more outstanding.

He locked eyes with her. "If I haven't said it yet, thank you."

"We make a good team, Reed." She frowned, her gaze

scanning his face. "Are you sure you're okay? Shouldn't you be checked out by a doctor?"

"I'm fine. Just bruised." His lips quirked. "I'm a lot tougher than I look."

"No one would think you weren't tough. Not for a moment."

The doors leading from the emergency room swung open and Austin walked out. His arm was in a sling and he favored his right leg.

Emma hopped up and gently hugged him. "What did the doctor say?"

Austin blushed as he pulled back. "It's nothing. My shoulder was dislocated, and I have a sprained ankle." His gaze jumped from Emma to Reed. "Molly?"

"She's going to make a full recovery, according to the doctors."

Austin let out a breath. "I'm glad. I saw Will going into Vernon's room with a defense attorney. Why aren't you in there interviewing him?"

"I decided it would be best to let Cooper take the lead on the case." Cooper Jackson was their local Texas Ranger. "It'll bump the case to a higher priority. Cooper can get the state lab to process the evidence quickly. Plus, he has the additional manpower to question witnesses faster than we can."

It would also free Reed up to personally guard Emma. The danger to her was growing exponentially.

Austin nodded. "Good idea. Cooper is an excellent investigator."

"What happened out there in the woods?" Reed asked.

"I went to the ridge to call in to headquarters when I overheard Vernon talking to someone. He didn't give a name, but he explicitly said the plan worked. He told the other person on the phone to hurry up."

Emma gasped. "I saw someone in the woods with a flashlight coming toward the cave. That's why I moved Molly closer to the rear entrance, out of sight. I assumed it was Vernon, but maybe I was wrong."

"Two criminals…" Reed rocked back on his heels. "On the night of the break-in at Emma's house, a truck nearly ran me off the road. It wasn't the man who actually attacked Emma because he was still in the house, but it could've been a getaway driver."

If there were two men working together all this time, that meant any alibis they'd collected were worthless. It put the case back at square one.

"There's more." Austin hesitated. "Vernon specifically said he didn't sign up for the murder part. If the other guy wanted you dead, he needed to move it."

Reed was standing close enough to feel the small tremor shake Emma's body. He slipped his hand into hers.

Austin grimaced. "I must've stepped on a branch or somehow given away my presence, because Vernon started shooting at me. I ended up rolling down the embankment."

The hospital doors swung open again. Will Norton, the county prosecutor, emerged. He was followed by Cooper. The Texas Ranger was scowling.

"I take it the questioning didn't go well," Reed said once the men were close enough.

Cooper snorted, running a hand through his shaggy hair. "Vernon isn't as stupid as his crimes might suggest."

"He pled the fifth and refused to answer any questions," Will said. "I've spoken with the defense attorney. I'll throw every charge I can at Vernon and ask for the maximum sentence for each one if he doesn't agree to cooperate. Murder-for-hire alone is a capital crime. He's going to discuss it with his client, but I'm not holding my breath."

Emma's shoulders sagged and Reed squeezed her hand.

"What about his phone? Since Austin heard him talking to someone—"

"We've recovered the cell phone, but it's locked." Cooper placed his hands on his hips, parting his sports jacket, revealing an oversize turquoise belt buckle. "Of course, Vernon refuses to unlock it for us or provide the password."

"We'll have to subpoena the records to see who he was talking to," Will said. "I've already had someone in my office start the paperwork. We should have it signed by a judge within the next couple of hours."

Reed let out a breath. Things were moving, but not fast enough. Whoever hired Vernon was still out there and free. What was to prevent him from trying to kill Emma a second time?

Emma sank into the seat of Reed's SUV. Exhaustion seeped into her muscles. She wanted a shower, some apple pie and a cuddle with her daughter. Sadie let out a sigh as she settled into the back seat.

The dome light didn't come on when Reed opened the driver's side door and climbed in. The engine rumbled to life. His strong hands held the wheel firmly, and his gaze flicked to the mirrors every so often as the hospital faded in the distance.

"You okay?" he asked.

"Emotionally drained, but otherwise I'm fine." She bit her lip. "Actually, I'm not fine. It was bad enough someone was stalking and trying to hurt me, but tonight Molly got caught in the cross fire. Vernon used his own daughter to set a trap for me."

"Which isn't your fault. You're not responsible for Vernon's actions."

"I know. Mentally, I get it. But I can't turn off my feelings so easily. I'm furious and I feel guilty. Molly's just a child, Reed. She didn't deserve what happened to her tonight."

He reached across the seat and took her hand. His palm was warm, the calluses rubbing lightly against the ridges of her knuckles. "You aren't the only one feeling that. I carry it, too. Maybe it's natural because of who we are."

Maybe it was. Reed's childhood had been marred by his father's abandonment and his mother's depression. Hers had been one of constant motion and chaos with new people and frequent moves. Circumstances had forced both of them into accepting responsibility for things outside of their control. It was a bond they'd shared as teenagers and, it seemed, now, as well.

"You did a good job tonight, Emma. You're tough." His mouth quirked up. "You'd make a fantastic law enforcement officer."

She laughed and wiped a stray tear from her cheek. "No, thank you. I'm much better at Search and Rescue."

"Don't tell Sadie, but I'm sure I owe her three boxes of biscuits now."

"You don't have to tell her. She's keeping score, I guarantee it."

He squeezed her hand. "I promise, Emma, we will get to the bottom of this."

"I know you will."

But what would be the cost until then? She trusted Reed to protect her and her family, but he wasn't invincible. He couldn't prevent everything or be everywhere at once. Tonight had been a close call. If Reed hadn't been wearing his bulletproof vest, things would've ended very differently. Just the thought of it sent her heart into overdrive.

Beyond the windshield, Emma could see the lights of her home winking through the trees. Her daughter would be asleep now, nestled in her bed, along with her stuffed lamb. Should they leave town? Abandon Helping Paws? The idea was gut-wrenching but there was more to consider than just herself. She had a daughter to protect.

Lord, please give me strength and guidance. Tell me what I'm supposed to do.

Reed squeezed her hand and she interlocked her fingers with his. A simple gesture and yet it brought her comfort. She wasn't in this alone.

Have faith. It was easy during good times. So much harder in the darker ones. Life was testing her, throwing curveballs she hadn't expected, but Emma had moved to Heyworth for a reason. She believed God was leading her. Maybe, just maybe, He'd sent Reed to help her through it.

The headlights picked up an object sailing through the night. It landed on the road in front of them. Emma blinked. Was that…a grenade?

"Reed!" she shouted.

He swerved. Emma's head slammed into the side of the SUV. A bright light preceded the sound of exploding glass. Then they were tumbling over and over.

Everything went black.

EIGHT

Awareness came slowly, like moving through a soupy fog. Reed smelled smoke and pine. His chest hurt. Something warm and wet swiped across his face.

He forced his eyes open. A tree branch was shoved through the shattered windshield. It took him far too long to realize he was upside down, his shoulder caught in the seat belt. The memories flashed like light bulbs. The grenade rolling into the road. His attempt to miss it. The explosion and the SUV rolling over. Emma's screams.

Emma. He twisted his head and was looking at a wall of fur. Sadie, freed from her seat belt in the collision, was blocking his view. "Emma, are you okay?"

She didn't respond. Reed fumbled for the seat belt release. For some mysterious reason, one of his headlights still functioned. The other was buried in the pine tree the vehicle had crashed into. Sadie licked the side of his face, her tongue leaving a wet trail. She had woken him. "Emma! Answer me!"

His fingers found the button and Reed pressed down. The seat belt gave way. He crashed in a heap onto the roof of the destroyed SUV. Glass shards cut into his pants and the palms of his hands.

He pushed Sadie out of the way. His breath caught.

Emma was unconscious. The side of her face was covered in blood. "Please, Lord, no."

Sadie whined. Deeply embedded training cut through the shock caused by the accident. With a shaking hand, he reached out and touched Emma's neck. The thump of her pulse was strong.

"Thank you, Lord."

His fingers searched and located a large gash hidden in her hair. Emma moaned. She needed help. She needed a hospital.

The extent of their problem wasn't just her injury. Whoever had thrown the grenade out into the road could still be nearby. Was he close enough to come after them? Reed wasn't willing to wait to find out.

Unfortunately his phone had been charging, tucked into the cup holder. Where was it?

Headlights lit up the car from behind. Reed froze. A car stopped on the side of the road. Friend or foe? He wasn't going to take any chances. Not with Emma. His heartbeat quickened and his fingers flew to his weapon, still holstered at his side. He maneuvered his body out of the broken window. Pain screamed from his ribs. Reed ignored it.

Footsteps crunched over the gravel shoulder. He circled to meet them, his gun leading the way.

"Police! Freeze, right there!" He ordered the figure shadowed by the headlights. "Not one more step."

The man immediately put his hands up to his shoulders. "Sheriff? It's me. Dean Shadwick. Don't shoot. I'm trying to help you."

Reed hesitated. "What are you doing here, Dean?"

"I… I was on my way home from town. I saw your vehicle on the side of the road."

"At two in the morning?"

"My mom lost her cat. She was in a panic, and I went to help her search for it."

Dean's ranch was two miles away, but this road was a shortcut from town. Reed lowered his weapon. "Did you see anyone else on the road?"

"No." His deputy took a deep breath. "What happened?"

"Someone attacked us. We need an ambulance and backup, now."

Hospitals were no place to get rest. Or decent food.

Emma poked her fork at the lump of mystery meat on her tray. They'd taken her vitals all night, the doctor keeping her for observation after the car accident. Her ribs were bruised, and she'd needed several stitches in her scalp. All in all, things could have been a whole lot worse.

She sampled the white glop masquerading as mashed potatoes. It tasted like ground plaster. Emma winced and pushed the food tray away.

"I'm pretty sure you're supposed to eat that," Vivian scolded. Dark circles marred the delicate skin under her sister-in-law's eyes, a testament to her own lack of sleep, and her blond hair was tucked into a sloppy ponytail. Lily bounced on her hip.

"It's not meant for human consumption." Emma lifted her daughter from Vivian's arms. Lily patted her cheek with a chubby hand. Emma grabbed it, planting a kiss on the soft palm. "Were you keeping your aunt up last night?"

"A bit. I think she's teething." Vivian held up the torn and bloody shirt Emma had been wearing yesterday—was it only just yesterday?—and blanched. "Of course, I wouldn't have gotten much sleep last night anyway."

The explosion had been close enough to the house, Vivian had heard it. Guilt pinched Emma. Vivian hadn't taken her brother's death well, and like Emma, she had very little extended family. As horrible as the situation was for Emma, it had to be worse for Vivian. She was left worrying. If the shoe was on the other foot—and Vivian was the one in danger—Emma would be frantic.

"You're a trooper, Vivi. Thank you for bringing new clothes and taking care of Lily. This would be so much worse if I didn't have you."

"Flattery will get you everywhere." Vivian grinned and tossed the destroyed shirt in the trash. "Of course, it would help me sleep better at night if we caught the guys doing this. Or even understood why they were after you. These attacks are extreme, and I can't believe it's simply to scare you off the property."

"I agree. Maybe Austin and Reed will have some news once they come back from the conference call with the Texas Ranger."

Vivian folded the pants Emma had been wearing last night before placing them in an overnight bag. "As crazy as it sounds, if a grenade had to be thrown at you, I'm glad Reed was there. The doctor said things would've been worse if Reed hadn't provided first aid and stopped the bleeding."

"I know." She'd regained consciousness as the EMTs were pulling her from the car. Reed stayed by her side the entire time, holding her hand. The first thing he did was assure Emma that Sadie was uninjured. "How was Sadie this morning?"

"Completely fine. The vet at the emergency clinic said to give her a couple of days rest. Deputy Irving walked her on a leash instead of letting her run loose in the yard this morning."

Lily bounced in Emma's arms and she winced. Vivian held out her hands. "Let me take her."

"No, I'm fine. Just a bit sore."

She was grateful to be alive. Grenades. Someone had actually thrown a grenade at their car. This situation had spiraled out of control so quickly, it made Emma's head spin. What had once been a couple of irritating incidents and creepy phone calls was turning into murder attempts and bombs.

The door to her room swung open. Reed strolled in. He'd showered and changed his clothes since the accident but hadn't shaved. The dark bristles on his jaw turned his eyes a deeper blue.

Austin followed his cousin into the room. His arm was still in a sling, but his gait was even, the sprained ankle clearly not bothering him anymore. His expression was as grim as Reed's. Emma chewed on the inside of her cheek. Whatever they'd found out from Cooper, the Texas Ranger, hadn't been good.

Reed spotted her full food tray and frowned. "Didn't the doctor say it was important for you to eat?"

"I tried to tell her the same." Vivian put her hands on her hips. "Maybe you can talk some sense into her."

"Don't start, either of you. The doctor has already cleared me to go home and that—" Emma waved a hand toward the offensive tray "—is not what I would call food."

Austin picked up the unused knife and dipped it in the mashed potatoes. He grimaced. "Prisoners get better grub than this."

Emma shot a triumphant look at her sister-in-law. "See. I told you."

Reed laughed. "It must be bad if Austin isn't willing to eat it. I've never seen him turn down a meal."

Lily bounced again in Emma's arms and lifted her hands toward Reed. He obliged, swinging her up high. She giggled. Everyone in the room chuckled.

"Watch out, Reed, or she'll have you wrapped around her little finger," Austin said.

"Something tells me your warning is too late." Vivian picked up her purse from a chair. "I'm hungry, and I'm sure Emma is, too. Why don't I go across the street to the diner and pick us up something for lunch while we wait for the discharge paperwork?"

"I don't think it's a good idea for you to go outside the hospital," Emma said. The memory of the grenade rolling out into the road made a shiver run down her spine.

"I have to eat sometime. And so do you. We can't stay in here forever. Besides, the attacks have been solely focused on you."

"I know, but it doesn't hurt to take precautions."

"There's a café in the lower level of the hospital," Reed said. "They make the best roast beef sandwiches. I'll stay here with Emma, and Austin can escort Vivian."

Vivian shot a glance at the chief deputy. A blush stained her cheeks. "I'm sure Austin has better things to do than babysit me."

"I'm not babysitting you. I'm protecting you. There's a difference." Austin winked. "And if you'll buy me a cup of potato soup to go with my sandwich, then we'll consider it a good trade."

Vivian's blush deepened, and Emma smothered a smile. It seemed she wasn't the only one struggling to resist a handsome lawman. They all placed an order for food and Vivian and Austin left.

"How are you feeling?" Reed asked, his gaze scanning her head.

"I'm fine. A bit anxious to hear what you found out from Cooper."

He shifted Lily in his arms and picked up the baby's

favorite stuffed lamb from the bed. "He was able to confirm Vernon was hired to target you."

"How?"

"They located his girlfriend at a local bar, and she spilled the beans. She also confirmed that he wasn't working alone, although she doesn't know who hired him or who his partners are."

"Partners? More than one person was hired to kill me?" She wrapped her arms around herself. "The man in the woods holding the flashlight wasn't the killer after all. He was another hired gun."

Reed nodded. "That's my guess. But there's more, Emma. It wasn't an accident that Vernon waited for me to come back to the cave. Or that the grenade was launched at my vehicle. Vernon's girlfriend said he would get a bonus if he took me out as well as you."

She sucked in a sharp breath. "But…that doesn't make any sense. Why would anyone target you and me?"

"There's only one reason I can think of. This is about Bonnie, Emma. This is all about my sister."

Reed grabbed Emma's arm. She'd gone pale, and he silently berated himself for the blunt delivery of his theory. She'd survived a grenade and shooting attack only yesterday.

Emma's long hair hung down her back, hiding the lump and stitches he knew were there. The silky strands brushed against his skin. "Maybe you should sit down."

She backed up until her knees hit the bed. "I don't understand. How is Bonnie's disappearance linked to these attacks?"

"This is going to sound far-fetched, but I think she's alive and being held captive somewhere. It's common knowledge in town that I've never given up on finding my sister."

Her eyes widened. "Sadie and I are a threat because we could make it possible to find Bonnie."

"Before you moved to Heyworth, the closest SAR canine was three hours away. It's the only thing that makes sense and explains why both you and I are being targeted."

His shoulders tensed as the silence stretched out between them. Reed half expected her to say he'd lost his mind, that grief was causing him to wish for things that weren't true. After all, he didn't have evidence proving Bonnie was the link. Nor could he prove she was alive. Not yet, anyway.

Emma lifted her gaze to meet his. The color had returned to her cheeks and there was a determined tilt to her chin. "I think it's time you tell me what happened to Bonnie."

He let out the breath he was holding. "When my sister initially went missing, the former sheriff believed she'd merely left town for a while. He had good reason to. A suitcase and clothes were missing from her apartment. Her purse and cell phone were gone, and so was her car. Our mom had died six months before. My sister's best friend, Margaret, confirmed Bonnie wasn't taking it well."

"But you didn't believe she'd run off?"

"No. The day she went missing, Bonnie called me and left a message. She wanted to talk about something important."

"Did she say what?"

"No, and when I tried to call her back hours later, she didn't answer."

Bonnie had already gone missing by then. Reed's stomach twisted painfully. He would give anything to go back to that moment and answer his phone when she called, but he'd been questioning the suspect of a double homicide at the time.

"Twenty-four hours went by and she still wasn't answering. I knew immediately something wasn't right. Bonnie would never ignore me. Especially after leaving a voice mail that asked me to call her back ASAP. I came straight to Heyworth and started digging into the case myself."

Lily stuck her thumb in her mouth and rested her head against Reed's shoulder. He ran a hand down her back and swayed. "I questioned several of her friends and found out Bonnie had been having a secret relationship with Joshua."

Emma's eyes widened. "Joshua Lowe? My neighbor?"

He nodded. "Bonnie hadn't told me about it. Probably because my sister knew I wouldn't approve. Joshua is bad news. He's done time for theft. Supposedly, he cleaned up his act and is on the straight and narrow path, but that's a recent turn around. Still too early in my opinion to know whether it's true or not."

"Do you think he had something to do with Bonnie's disappearance?"

"I think it's a strong possibility. On the night Bonnie went missing, she and Joshua were running away to elope."

Emma frowned. "That's why she packed a suitcase."

"Exactly. Joshua claims he arrived at the meeting place late and she wasn't there. But he can't provide me with an alibi." Reed shifted his hold on Lily, careful not to wake the sleeping baby. "To complicate matters, Bonnie worked as a paralegal for Judge Norton. She and Will had been dating but broke up shortly before she got involved with Joshua."

Emma's head was spinning with all of the information. Will Norton was the county prosecutor. He was also Judge Norton's nephew.

"Hold on, let me make sure I understand everything,"

she said. "Will Norton and Bonnie were dating. They broke up. After that, Bonnie and Joshua started dating."

"Right."

"Bonnie and Joshua got serious and were planning to elope. They set up a meeting and, according to Joshua, Bonnie never showed."

"Yes. Will told me that he and Bonnie met for lunch on the day of her disappearance. They were talking about getting back together."

"If that's true, why did she pack a suitcase?"

"My guess is Bonnie didn't know what to do. That could be why she called me. Bonnie and I often gave each other advice."

"I remember you were very close." Emma tapped her fingers against her lips. "Okay, so Bonnie packs a bag, goes to the meeting place and…what? She tells Joshua she can't go through with marrying him?"

"Or Bonnie told him she still had feelings for Will. Either way, I don't think the meeting went the way Joshua wanted it to and there was an altercation between them."

"Where were they supposed to meet?" she asked.

"At Franklin Park on the edge of town. Her cell phone was recovered from the park, smashed into pieces. Her car, purse and suitcase are still missing."

"What about Bonnie's phone records?"

"They show Joshua tried calling her several times on the night she disappeared, but that doesn't prove anything. He's had run-ins with the law in the past. He knew we'd check her phone. It's possible he called Bonnie to bolster his own story."

"But you can't prove it."

"No." He drew in a deep breath. "While Joshua doesn't have an alibi, there's no physical evidence linking him to the crime. The former sheriff never took the case seriously.

Leads weren't tracked down. By the time I was elected to take his place, the trail had gone cold."

She rose from the bed and placed a hand on his arm. "Reed, that's awful. I'm so sorry. I can't imagine how painful this has been for you."

Emma's touch was comforting, but it was the warmth and understanding in the depths of her gorgeous eyes that was Reed's undoing. Time had changed them both, given them pain and edges. But it hadn't shifted Emma's bravery or kindness. Standing there, with Lily in his arms, he felt the wall closing off his heart cracking.

"I always took my cases seriously, Emma. Always. But being on the other side…it changes everything."

"Of course it does." She met his gaze. "It seems I'm not the only one God gave a mission to."

"No, although it's difficult to understand why Bonnie had to go missing to make it happen."

She touched Lily's back. "I don't know why Mark had to die either, but there are some things at work bigger than us. We need to have faith, as hard as it is."

"You don't think I'm crazy to believe Bonnie might be alive?"

"There is nothing wrong with holding out hope, Reed. I've worked search-and-rescue cases when things looked bleak. Either the person had been missing for a long time or the weather was terrible. Wonderful things happen. I've seen it, and if there's a chance Bonnie is alive, then we have to try to find her." She leaned closer. "You said yesterday I wasn't in this by myself. Well, you aren't either. If there's any way Sadie and I can help, then we will."

He reached out and cupped Emma's face with his hand. Her skin was soft. Reed ran his thumb over the crest of her cheek. His breath caught as Emma's gaze drifted to his mouth and lingered.

He wanted to kiss her. Desperately. The spark created when they were eighteen still lingered, their connection unchanged by time or distance.

He was a fool. Reed knew that now. He'd tried to avoid it, tried to keep her squarely in the friend zone, but his heart didn't know how to resist her special brand of compassion and strength. She was his own personal kryptonite.

His thumb swept across the line of her lower lip. Emma inhaled. Their eyes locked in and time stood still. She edged closer.

The ground shook under their feet as a blast of light blinded them. The explosion rattled the windowpane with the force of an earthquake. Reed grabbed Emma. Tucking Lily between them, he used his body to block them from the glass.

The lights in the hospital went out.

NINE

"Reed, that was some kind of explosion." There was a faint tremble in Emma's voice, so soft, anyone else would've missed it. "Could it have been a transformer? Is that why the lights went out?"

"Possibly." Reed didn't say it, but he didn't have to. Emma was smart enough to realize it could also be the second attacker, Grenade Man. "Any moment, the backup generators should kick on. Here, take Lily."

Reed transferred the baby to her arms. Thankfully, the explosion hadn't woken Lily, and he was careful not to either. Whatever was happening, it would be better if the baby slept through it. "Hold on to the back of my shirt, Emma."

His mind was racing but he kept his voice calm and controlled. He turned. Emma grabbed the fabric of his shirt with a tight hold. Reed pulled his weapon. "Vernon is still here in the hospital. He's under guard, but he's one floor above us."

"If that was a bomb, he didn't plant it. But his partner may be trying to break him out."

The room was pitch-black except for a faint light coming in from the window. It appeared the entire hospital had lost power.

He waited a moment. Two. The hospital's backup generator didn't kick in. Probably because the explosion had taken it out. There was no way this was a coincidence. Grenade Man was back and either desperate or determined enough to make an attack on the hospital. Who was this guy?

He pulled out his cell and shot off a text to Austin and Deputy Kyle Hendricks. Both were in this hospital somewhere—Austin with Vivian, Kyle with Vernon—and Reed had to be sure they reacted accordingly. He also sent a text to his dispatch operator, asking for backup, before pocketing his phone.

Behind him, Emma's breathing was rapid and shaky. She was whispering something. A prayer.

"Emma, listen to me, I'm taking you and Lily out of here." He reached behind him with his free hand and squeezed her arm. "Follow closely behind me, keeping your hand on my shirt and Lily in between us. You got that?"

"But what about Vivian?" Her voice rose an octave. "She's—"

"Austin will get her to safety. Don't worry about Vivian right now. Your job is to stay safe for Lily."

"Got it." The words were followed by another quick prayer. It touched him to hear her whisper his name. He found himself sending up a prayer of his own.

Lord, please, help me protect this woman and her young child. I care about them. I don't want them hurt.

He did care about them. More than he wanted to admit. Yet, those emotions were also dangerous. If he didn't give the case everything he had, mistakes would be made. People could be killed.

His job was to protect Emma and Lily. He had every intention of doing just that.

Behind him, Emma's breathing slowed slightly as she shored up her courage. Reed let go of her arm and eased forward. He reached for the door handle. It was cool to the touch. He swung it open, leading with his weapon.

The hall was in a state of pandemonium. Doctors and nurses scrambled while machines in various rooms beeped and a cacophony of voices came from patients and family members. Emergency lights glowed from the ceiling. The coverage was spotty and created long shadows big enough to hide an elephant in.

Reed didn't like this. He didn't like it at all. Leaving the room exposed them but staying was worse. Without knowing how many hitmen were on the killer's payroll, Reed couldn't be sure of their plan. No, it was better to get Emma and Lily to a secure location.

He scanned the hallway, but no one was focused on them. Reed lowered his gun slightly—no sense in terrifying people more than they already were—and moved toward the stairway at the end of the hall. It was the farthest away, but his vehicle was parked in the garage right next to it, making for a quicker escape.

Emma did as he asked. She was close enough he could feel Lily's small body pressed against his back.

Faint pops echoed from somewhere in the building. Reed paused.

"Are those gunshots?" Emma breathed out.

"Yes." Vernon was on the floor above him. Either he was making an escape attempt or he was being rescued.

Lord, if you're listening, please also watch over my men. Help them do their jobs and give us the strength and courage to protect the innocent civilians depending on us.

Reed stopped a nurse passing by them, pointing to his sheriff's badge. "Grab your staff and initiate the protocol for a shooter in the building."

Her eyes widened for a moment and then she rushed to a nearby doctor. Reed stayed underneath an emergency light so he was visible. The doctor glanced at him, took in his badge and the gun in his hand, before quickly picking up a nearby phone.

An emergency code sounded over the PA system, alerting the rest of the hospital. The flurry of activity increased as staff started gathering patients and family members into rooms. Protocol was to lock them in.

More faint pops sounded. He needed to get Emma out of here. Now.

"Come on." He quickened his steps toward the staircase. The door swung into the cavernous space. Empty. Reed tried to keep his footsteps soft, but the sound echoed off the concrete floor and walls. Five floors. That's how far they had to go to access the parking lot.

He activated the light on his weapon. "Stay close."

Emma gave a sharp nod. Her jaw was tight with fear, but her eyes reflected determination. Lily, thankfully, stayed sleeping against her mother's shoulder. Reed steadied his breath and locked down his worry about them. It wouldn't serve him. He moved as quickly as he could without tripping Emma. One floor down.

Faster. Faster.

The urgency in his gut was matched only by Emma's breathing. Another floor down.

Below them, a door opened. Reed froze.

Emma's heart leaped as the door slammed shut in the stairwell below them. Reed's back went rigid before immediately relaxing. Not because the threat had passed. No, because danger was coming straight for them, and he wanted to be ready.

As if echoing her thoughts, Reed maneuvered her and

Lily between him and the wall. The cool banister bit into her back. Reed's wide shoulders cut off her view. The light from his gun allowed her only the faintest glimpse of his shirt.

He wasn't wearing a vest.

The thought sliced through her. Panic threatened to well up and choke her. Only moments ago she'd nearly kissed this man. Now they were under attack. Reed might die protecting her and her daughter. She'd already lost her husband. Would she lose another man she was growing to care about? It seemed impossible but Emma tightened her hold on Reed's shirt. The fabric cut into her fingers.

Please, Lord, keep us safe.

Silence echoed in the stairwell. The only sound was Emma's heartbeat pounding in her ears. Where was the person who'd entered the stairwell? With every ticking moment, the intensity of their situation pulled her muscles tighter. Maybe it was another patient? Or family member? The hospital was on lockdown but that didn't necessarily mean someone hadn't wanted to leave instead. But then, why wasn't the person moving?

Lily wriggled slightly in her arms. Her lashes fluttered open. No, no, no.

Baby girl, don't wake up.

If Lily started crying or talking, it would attract attention. Emma gently rocked her and the baby's eyes closed again. She sighed back into sleep.

Reed jerked his head to the side and gently tugged on Emma with his free hand. He wanted her to move toward the door right above them. She eased out from between Reed and the wall, careful to keep her footsteps light.

Something whistled past her ear. Concrete exploded behind her. Someone was shooting at them! Fear drove

Emma to quicken her steps, no longer concerned with staying quiet. All she wanted was safety.

"I know you're there." A man's voice from below echoed through the stairwell. "Don't make this harder than it has to be."

Another shot whizzed past her. Emma nearly screamed.

"Go, Emma," Reed encouraged. "Faster."

She increased her pace up the stairs. Reed was right behind her, keeping her body covered with his own. Emma shoved open the door and launched herself into the hospital hallway. Pounding footsteps were coming up the stairwell. Reed slammed the door shut. It provided some protection from the shooter and bought them precious seconds.

Emma ran down the hall. Her chest was tight and her head throbbed. There was no way they could outrun this guy. The hospital was devoid of people. The minute he came up the stairs, he would spot them. Reed grabbed her arm, stopping her momentum. "In here."

He pushed Emma and Lily inside an open supply closet before shutting the door behind them. Racks of medical supplies towered above her. It smelled of bleach and laundry detergent. She turned, the metallic taste of fear filling her mouth when she realized Reed wasn't with them. He'd stayed in the hall to confront the shooter.

A man shouted, voice muffled through the door, "Where is she? The dog lady?"

Dog lady. There was no doubt these guys were looking for her. And anyone around her was immediately put at risk. The patients and their families. Reed.

Lily.

Fresh adrenaline raced through her veins. Lily couldn't be found with her. Emma searched for a place to stash her daughter. She scrambled to the back of the closet, grabbing some towels along the way. The bottom rack held rolls of toilet paper. She shoved them out of the way and spread the towels on the shelf like a makeshift bed. She quickly pressed a kiss to her daughter's face before laying her down.

"Stay sleeping, pretty girl. Mommy will be right back."

She rapidly restacked the toilet paper in front of the baby to hide her. Emma scanned the room again, this time looking for any kind of weapon. Not that much could be used against a gun. Still, something had to be better than nothing.

A mop caught her eye. She removed the stick. Keeping it gripped in her hands, she moved back to the door.

"I'm with the Heyworth County Sheriff's Department. Put your gun on the ground and your hands in the air."

Reed's tone was authoritative and strong. For the second time in two days, he was negotiating with a man holding a gun while innocent civilians were within range.

"Where is she?" the other man screamed. "I will tear this floor apart looking for her, shooting everyone along the way, Sheriff. Have no doubt. You have thirty seconds to produce her. Now!"

No. Emma wouldn't allow that to happen. She couldn't. Her hand reached for the door handle. It was cold against her skin. She paused. Waiting.

Please, Lord. Have him put down the gun.

Shots rang out. Emma jumped.

Had Reed been shot? Her breath caught in her throat and she strained to hear something beyond the door. Nothing. Tears pricked her eyes. She forced them back. It wasn't time to fall apart. Not yet—

The doorknob rattled under her hand and she shrieked.

"Emma, open up. It's Reed."

She flung the door open. He stood in front of her, whole

and unharmed. Her relief and panic must've shown in her expression because Reed gathered her into his arms.

"It's over. The man who attacked us is dead."

Her body shook as tears swept over her cheeks. She couldn't bring herself to pull it together. Voices rose up behind Reed. A radio crackled.

"Building secure…"

His hand rubbed up and down on her back. When her sobs subsided, she pulled back a bit. "I'm always crying on you."

"I don't mind." His thumb wiped away a straggling tear. "Where's Lily?"

"I hid her behind the toilet paper." Emma realized she was still holding the mop stick. "I didn't want him to find her…" Her voice trailed off. She couldn't finish the thought.

"Good thinking, Em." Reed passed her and crouched down. He uncovered Lily in record time. The baby giggled when he lifted her. It nearly set off Emma's tears again.

She swallowed hard. "Vivian?"

"She's safe. They'll meet us at the car."

Emma let out a whoosh of air. "What happened?"

"The attacker wanted to find you," Reed said. "He needed me to tell him where you were. When I didn't, he shot toward the nursing station. There were some people hiding there. I had to shoot him."

His words were flat. Harsh even. But Emma didn't have to be told why. He was keeping his own emotions bottled up tight. He'd saved lives, but Emma was under no illusions that it didn't come at a cost.

"The man who attacked us wasn't alone," Reed continued. "Someone else was helping Vernon escape."

Two men. Just like in the woods. Emma's throat tightened. "Did they get away? Was anyone hurt?"

"Vernon was shot, but his accomplice escaped." Reed held her daughter tenderly and took Emma's hand. "The building's secure, but we need to get you out of here. We're going back down the stairs, this time escorted by some of my men."

She nodded, and they stepped out. The hospital floor was crawling with deputies. Emma focused on the feel of Reed's hand in her own to calm her nerves. His grip was strong but also gentle. This time they traversed the stairs without a problem. The parking garage was full of vehicles. Reed had procured a new official vehicle from the department's spares. It sat in the fire lane next to another patrol car. Vivian popped out, running toward them.

Emma embraced her sister-in-law. Vivian gripped her tight enough to cut off her breathing.

"Ladies, let's get into the car," Reed said. "Now."

The tone of his voice alerted Emma to the fact that while the immediate threat was over, the danger wasn't. There was an attacker still out there. Somewhere. She climbed into the back seat. Reed deposited Lily into a car seat he'd obviously put in to bring the baby and Vivian to the hospital earlier. Emma busied her hands by strapping her daughter in good and tight.

Reed drove out of the parking garage. Lily pointed at something outside of the window and babbled. Desperate for normalcy, Emma tweaked her nose. "What are you looking at? What do you see?"

Emma glanced out the window. A flash of fabric caught her eye. A man with blond hair; a familiar gait.

Her cousin, Owen.

Running from the direction of the hospital.

TEN

Hours after the attack at the hospital, Reed's heartbeat was still working on settling itself into a normal rhythm. He'd driven Emma and her family to the only place he could guarantee they were safe—his own sheriff's department. Encasing them behind a wall of deputies allowed him to focus on the threats against them.

The bull pen was like a humming beehive. Deputies flowed in and out, phones rang, and keyboards clattered as Reed walked through. He entered the break room and went straight for the coffeepot. Several boxes from a local pizzeria were stacked on the table. Reed's stomach rumbled, and he snagged a slice to have with his coffee.

The blinds in his office were open. Vivian played on the floor with Lily using some blocks and foam cups she'd unearthed from somewhere. Emma spotted him through the glass and joined him in the break room. Sadie followed her mistress.

"Are you okay?" Reed asked. He took a new cup and poured some coffee for her.

"As good as can be expected." She rubbed her forehead. "But between you and me, I'm still shaken. This attack was a close call for Lily and Vivian."

His jaw tightened. "Too close. Not just for them, but for you, as well."

Thankfully, no innocent people had been hurt. Still, the weight of taking another man's life weighed heavily on Reed's shoulders. He didn't regret it. His decision had saved innocent lives. He just wished it hadn't come to that.

Emma took the coffee from him and their fingers brushed. A jolt of electricity arced through the air. His gaze dropped to her lips, remembering the moments before the explosion. Would they have kissed? Most likely.

Reed gave himself a mental shake. His train of thought was completely ill timed and inappropriate considering everything going on.

"Is there anything new?" She stirred some milk into her coffee. "Or some way I can help? I'm going a bit stir-crazy."

He didn't blame her. If he'd been sitting in a room for the last several hours, he'd be itching to do something, too. "I'm about to have a meeting with Austin and Cooper to go over what we know so far. Why don't you join us?"

Having another set of eyes wouldn't hurt. Emma had proven herself to be more than capable of handling tense situations. Besides, it was her life being threatened and her family caught in the cross fire. Reed didn't see any point in holding back information from her.

"Okay," Emma said. "Let me just tell Vivi where I'll be."

He took his coffee and went into the conference room. Austin and Cooper were already waiting inside. So was Will Norton. As the county prosecutor, it made sense for him to stay up to date on their investigation. A whiteboard stretched along one wall, various photographs and notes arranged in an organized fashion.

Reed greeted the men and took a chair on the far side

so he had a clear view of the board. "Let's go over what we do know, from the beginning."

The conference room door opened. Emma and her dog slipped inside the room. She took the chair next to him. Her vanilla scent tickled his nose and soothed something inside him. He liked having her close.

Austin stood up. "We've officially identified two of the suspects from the hospital. Vernon Hanks, you know. He was killed outside the hospital while trying to escape."

Reed's heart twisted. Not for Vernon but for his daughter. To lose a father under any circumstances was hard, but this was so much worse. Molly deserved better. Thankfully, she had her mother and stepfather to rely on.

"The man you shot…" Austin took a photo down off the board and slid it across the table to Reed "…was Vernon's cousin, Charlie Young."

Reed frowned. "That name sounds familiar."

"It should." Will smoothed a hand down his tie. This one was dark blue and matched his pinstriped suit. "He lives in Heyworth and has a rap sheet a mile long. Started out in petty theft and minor drug dealing, but over the years, he's worked himself up to aggravated assault. Got out of jail a few months ago."

The man at the hospital had been wearing a ski mask, so Reed hadn't gotten a good look at him. Charlie's mug shot showed a thin-faced individual with stringy hair. Reed remembered the same image had crossed his desk a few weeks ago. "Wasn't there an arrest warrant issued for him last month for skipping parole?"

Will nodded. "Yep. He'd gone underground, and supposedly, no one's heard from him. But you know how that is."

Deputies would've gone to Charlie's last known address, talked to his family and friends regarding his whereabouts. But with career criminals, police often got the runaround. Reed pushed the photo over to Emma so she could get a better look. "Ever seen this guy before?"

She studied it for a long moment before shaking her head. "No. Not that I recall."

Austin slid over another photograph. "This is Vernon's other cousin. Mike Young. The younger brother of Charlie."

Reed could easily see the family resemblance. Same beady eyes, same greasy hair.

"I've never seen this guy either." Emma leaned over to see the photograph better. "You think this is the other guy from the hospital? The one that got away?"

"It's impossible to know for sure until we find and question him. But my guess would be yes. Mike did a stint in the military for a while. He specialized in explosives."

Beside him, Emma inhaled sharply. Reed eyed the photograph with renewed interest. There was little doubt Mike Young was Grenade Man. "That bumps him to the top of our suspect list."

"We've got every officer in the state looking for him." Cooper rested his arms on the table. The Texas Ranger had shed his sports jacket and rolled up the sleeves of his white button-down. "He won't be free for long."

"Any idea who hired them?"

Austin shook his head. "We're still working on that. We do know Charlie was the primary contact. We recovered his cell phone, and we were able to open it. There are text messages between Charlie and Mike talking about a $15,000 payment. Charlie was probably the one who broke into Emma's house. We conducted a search of his apartment and found both the missing tablet and the gold pen."

Reed mulled that over for a moment. "Okay, so someone tries to scare Emma off the property, and when that doesn't work, he hires Charlie to break in. The initial plan was to make it appear as a home robbery that went wrong. Except I showed up."

"Agreed. When that failed, Charlie pulled in his brother and Vernon to help out."

Emma was pale, and her fingers trembled. She was keeping it together, but Reed knew inside she was freaking out. Finding out you were the victim of a murder-for-hire wasn't easy for anyone, but it was far worse for a woman who'd already lost a husband and had a baby depending on her.

Reed placed a hand on her arm. "You okay?"

She took a deep breath. "It's okay. I want to hear everything."

Reed gestured for Austin to continue, but it was Cooper who spoke. "We found evidence confirming what Vernon's girlfriend told us. The burner phone Charlie had on him contained clear instructions. Emma was to be killed. The fee was double if you were taken out, as well."

"Do we know when that decision was made?"

"After the break-in at Emma's house failed. Essentially, when you took over the case."

Reed sat back in his chair. "The only connection I can think of is Bonnie."

"Hold on." Cooper held up a hand. "We don't have a shred of physical evidence indicating these recent attacks are connected to your sister's disappearance."

"What else could it be?" Emma asked.

"Well, Reed has a reputation for being thorough and determined. Once he was involved, the perpetrator likely knew he wouldn't let it go. Especially if you were murdered. Taking him out along with you does two things. It muddies the investigation and removes, at least in the perpetrator's mind, the one person who would go to the ends of the earth to get justice."

Reed hated to admit it, but Cooper's logic made sense. "So you're suggesting we focus on Emma. We need to uncover why someone would want her out of the way."

"Precisely. Since this entire thing started with someone trying to run Emma out of town, I'm inclined to believe this has less to do with her and more to do with her land." Cooper leaned forward. "Emma, you're building a search-and-rescue canine training facility. Maybe there's something on your property the perpetrator is trying to prevent you from finding."

Her eyes widened. "Something we might stumble on by accident while training the dogs or while making improvements to the land."

"Exactly. It has to be big enough it can't be moved or it has to be something that couldn't be moved without people noticing."

Reed's stomach sank. There was only one person he could think of who had a vested interest in hiding something on Emma's property. "We haven't located Owen yet, have we?"

Owen had been in the hospital because of an adverse reaction to some medication he'd been given for treatment of Sadie's bite. He'd been under guard, but the ensuing confusion during the attack had enabled him to escape.

"Not yet," Cooper said. "We need to consider that Owen may be the one who hired the hitmen. While we're looking for him, I recommend we conduct a search of Emma's property. Uncovering what's hidden there may be the best way to keep everyone safe."

Reed nodded, squeezing Emma's arm. Her face was pale, worry lines etched in the curve of her brow. She'd never been very good at hiding her emotions. The same concerns running through his mind were written in her expression.

When they conducted a search of Emma's property, what would they find?

By dinnertime, Emma's body ached and her head was pounding. The pain was exacerbated by the swirling emotions inside her. Could Owen really have hired hitmen to kill her? Where would he have gotten the money? A small part of her clung to the notion that there was no way her cousin was behind this. It seemed ridiculous, given his actions, but she couldn't quite let herself believe Owen wanted her dead.

The search of her property would start tomorrow morning. Until they uncovered what was hidden, she was a target. The first order of business was getting her family out of harm's way.

Reed punched a code into his phone, and the gates to his aunt's ranch opened. The SUV bounced over the cattle guard.

"Gorgeous sunset," Vivian remarked from the back seat. Deep purples and streaks of pink played across the wide-open sky. The driveway curved and the house came into view. It was two stories with a large wraparound porch. "And a lovely house."

"You'll like Aunt Bessie," Emma said. "She's one of the sweetest people I've ever met."

Emma lifted Lily out of her car seat. Lily waved at Reed's aunt as she hurried down the porch steps to greet them. Everything about Aunt Bessie was soft, from the pale peach dress fluttering around her calves to the silver hair swept back in a bun at the nape of her neck.

"Welcome, welcome." Bessie introduced herself to Vivian before patting Reed's cheek. "Take the suitcases to the blue room, dear."

Bessie hugged Austin, careful to avoid jostling her son's shoulder, before turning her attention to Emma and Lily. "Emma, your daughter is beautiful. She looks just like you."

"Until she scowls. Then she looks like her daddy."

Bessie laughed. "Well, we are gonna do our best to prevent any scowls, aren't we, sweet Lily?"

Lily grinned and babbled in response. Sadie, freed from the car, bounded over. Reed's aunt greeted her with a pat to the head. "Hello, sweetness."

Emma bent down to kiss the older woman's cheek. "Thank you for letting Vivian and Lily stay here."

"Nonsense." Bessie wrapped an arm around Emma's waist, steering her toward the house. "Y'all are doing me a favor. It gets lonely knocking around this old house by myself."

Crossing the threshold was like stepping back in time. The leather recliner, its color worn away in places, still sat in the living room next to the L-shaped sofa. The wood cabinet holding the television gleamed in the waning sunlight. It smelled of yeasty bread and cinnamon. Emma's stomach growled.

"I hope y'all brought your appetites with you," Bessie declared. "I've made fried chicken and all the sides, including buttermilk biscuits. Dinner will be ready in fifteen. Emma, love, you remember where the blue room is, don't you?" She waited for Emma's nod. "Go on and show Vivian where she and Lily will be staying. Reed, I need your help digging the high chair out of the garage."

Emma waved for Vivian to follow her down the hall. From the kitchen Bessie's voice bellowed, "Austin Joseph

Carter, get your grubby mitts away from my biscuits and start setting the table."

Emma and Vivian burst out laughing at the way Bessie scolded her grown son. There weren't many who probably spoke to the chief deputy that way. Lily also laughed. Some of the weight on Emma's shoulders seemed to dissipate. Aunt Bessie's house was like a bubble of warmth.

"You're right," Vivian whispered between chuckles. "I love her already."

"I knew you would."

Her sister-in-law paused by a photograph hanging in the hall. "That's you with Reed."

Emma backed up a few steps. Sure enough, a younger version of herself and Reed were sitting on Aunt Bessie's porch. Bonnie, her short hair tousled by the wind, was pointing to the checkerboard between them, probably giving advice. Austin stood behind Reed, his arms crossed over his chest.

"I remember this," Emma said. "We were having a checkers competition."

"Did you spend a lot of time here?"

"Not a lot, but some." Reed and Bonnie would spend days with Aunt Bessie when their mother's depression got to be too much. Emma tagged along, happy to be anywhere Reed was. "We always had a good time. Uncle Jeb and Aunt Bessie's late husband were good friends, so it was a natural fit."

They stepped into the blue room, aptly named for the bluebonnet wallpaper. There was a sitting area with a television, an attached bathroom, and gorgeous floor-to-ceiling windows overlooking the backside of the ranch. Bessie had even set up a crib for Lily.

"This is beautiful." Vivian walked over to the window. "And peaceful. I can see why you spoke so highly of it."

"It's a good place to stay under any circumstance, but it's a real blessing now. A state trooper will be assigned to watch the house. You and Lily will be safe here."

Vivian took a deep breath. "I wish you were staying, too. Please promise me you'll be careful."

"Of course. Reed's already said he's going to be glued to my side."

Lily fussed, so Emma placed the baby on the carpet. Sadie sniffed her and Lily laughed before crawling away to explore the room. Emma kept one eye on her.

"Glued to your side, huh?" Vivian's eyes twinkled. "Any chance the sparks I've noticed between the two of you will develop into something more?"

"Vivian!"

"What? It's a nice break from all this murder and mayhem. So, spill the beans."

Emma's cheeks heated. "We… Well, I think Reed was about to kiss me."

Vivian's face broke out into a grin. "Oh, really? When did this happen?"

"At the hospital. Before the attack." Emma picked at an invisible piece of lint before straightening her shirt.

Her sister-in-law's gleeful expression faded into something more serious. "What's the problem, Emma? I know you like him."

"Yes, but with all of this murder and mayhem, as you put it, I don't think now is the best time to complicate the relationship."

"Oh, hon, it's the only way you would've broken out of your shell. Don't get me wrong. I'm not wishing for your life to be in danger, but you were in a rut and determined to stay there. It was clear to me from the beginning there was something between you and Reed. If this brings the two of you closer together, then I'm glad some good came out of all of this ugliness."

"I hadn't thought of it that way." Emma paused. "But to be honest, we agreed to be friends. Maybe it's a good thing the kiss didn't happen. He might've regretted it."

"Or he might not have. You won't know until you talk to him about it. Something tells me that Reed doesn't act without thinking and my guess is, he's just as worried about rocking the boat as you are."

Vivian had a point. Still, things were a mess at the moment. Emma didn't want to say it, but she wasn't entirely sure she wanted to risk her heart again. Reed had a dangerous job. She'd already lost her husband. Could she fall in love again knowing the pain that would come if tragedy struck? Emma wasn't sure she had it in her.

A knock came from the doorway. Reed stuck his head in. "Hey, ladies, dinner is ready."

"Great. I'm starving." Vivian scooped up Lily. The little girl protested, and she bounced her a bit. "Let's go see what Aunt Bessie has for us."

Emma followed behind a bit slower. Reed greeted her with a smile that warmed the depths of his blue eyes. Her steps faltered. She mentally shook herself. Now was not the time to be gooey over Reed. Even if the man had saved her life and that of her daughter's. Several times.

"Thanks for arranging this," Emma said. "I think Vivian and Lily are going to have a good time with your aunt."

"So do I. And it'll make me feel better to know they're out of harm's way."

"Me, too."

He placed a hand on the small of her back as they walked down the hall toward the dining room. The warmth of his touch spread through her and reinforced Vivian's words. Eventually, Emma and Reed would have to discuss their relationship.

But now wasn't the time.

ELEVEN

The next morning, Reed rose at daybreak. His house was quiet. The doors to both his spare bedrooms were still closed. Emma was in one, Austin in the other. A deputy was patrolling Emma's property, but Reed didn't feel comfortable staying in her home given the circumstances. His house had a security system including an alarm and cameras. It would be a lot harder for anyone to sneak up on them.

He started the coffee and breakfast. Twenty minutes later, Austin joined him in the kitchen.

"Smells good." Austin said a quick prayer before snagging a piece of toast. "If I'd known breakfast was part of the bargain, I would've been a houseguest a long time ago."

Reed snorted. "Don't get used to it. How's your shoulder?"

"Better. Still a bit sore, but at least I can lose the sling now." Austin glanced at his watch. "You got a to-go cup for the coffee? I want to get over to Emma's property before the rest of the troops show up. It'll give me time to organize the search."

"Sure thing. Emma and I will be over soon."

"Take your time. After all she's been through, I'm sure she needs the sleep."

Austin ate quickly and left. The click of Sadie's nails on the tile flooring preceded the dog's appearance in the kitchen. Emma followed. Her hair was pulled into a simple braid. She hadn't put on any makeup and was dressed for hiking in jeans along with a lightweight long-sleeve shirt. "Morning."

Reed momentarily lost his words. Emma's beauty was striking, but it was nothing compared to the warmth and kindness shining in her eyes. "Uhhh, morning. Coffee?"

"Yes, please. Is the alarm off? I have to let Sadie out for a potty break and some exercise."

He poured a cup of coffee for her before topping off his own. "I'll come with you."

Outside, dew coated the grass in the yard. Reed took a deep breath of the fresh air and scanned the immediate area for any danger. Nothing stirred, except for a few birds flying overhead. Sadie trotted over to some bushes.

"Did you sleep well?" he asked Emma.

She took a sip of her coffee. "Better than well. I feel like a new person. I'm sure having two lawmen around, plus a full-scale security system had a lot to do with it. Has Austin already left?"

"Yes, he wanted to get a jump start on the search."

The sound of a car caught Reed's attention and he turned. A sedan pulled to a stop in his driveway, a young woman behind the wheel. Reed recognized her instantly. Margaret Carpenter was the local veterinarian. She'd also been Bonnie's best friend.

"Is that Margaret?" Emma asked.

"Yep. Maybe she wants to check in on Sadie," Reed said, as he and Emma crossed the yard toward the driveway. "She was out of town when Deputy Irving called to have Sadie checked out after the grenade attack. Her answering service referred us to the vet in the next town. Have you ever met Margaret?"

"Briefly, when I first moved to town. I wanted to talk with her about providing care for the dogs at my training facility. She seemed really nice."

Margaret climbed out of the vehicle, dressed in scrubs. When he got close enough, Reed lifted the cup in his hand. "Hey, Margaret. Would you like to come in for some coffee?"

"No, thanks. I have to run to work, but I'm glad I caught you. I was away on a cruise with some girlfriends until last night. Will gave me an update on what's been going on and the possible connection to Bonnie's disappearance."

Reed's hand tightened on his coffee mug. Will shouldn't have shared that information with anyone. "I'm sorry, Margaret. I can't discuss an ongoing investigation." He was, however, going to have a long conversation with the county prosecutor. Will knew better.

"Don't be mad at Will, Reed. I heard rumors going around at the diner when I stopped in to grab a quick dinner and confronted him. He knew Bonnie and I were very close. It was only a matter of time before I got the information from the rumor mill anyway. Besides, I may have information that pertains to the case." Margaret's gaze darted toward Emma before settling back on Reed. "It's about Owen."

"Okay."

Margaret opened her mouth but hesitated. Emma gave her a reassuring smile. "It's all right. Tell us."

The other woman nodded. "Bonnie and Owen had an altercation a few months before she went missing."

Reed reared back. "What kind of altercation?"

"Owen had a case in front of Judge Norton. A DUI, I

think. Anyway, there was some kind of interaction between Owen and Bonnie outside the courtroom."

Judge Norton was only one of a handful of judges for the county, so it wasn't unusual for him to hear many of the cases from Heyworth. Bonnie had worked as Judge Norton's paralegal.

"Bonnie didn't get into specifics, but she made it sound like a normal, friendly conversation," Margaret continued. "Owen had gone to our high school and, although he was there as defendant, it wasn't in Bonnie's nature to be ugly to anyone."

"No, it wasn't. She always had a kind word for everyone," Reed said. A sharp ache settled in his chest, but he refused to acknowledge it. Instead, he focused on the conversation at hand. "What happened next?"

Margaret crossed her arms over her chest. "Owen waited for Bonnie to get off work and approached her in the parking lot of the courthouse. He repeatedly asked her out. When she refused, Owen became enraged. He called her a flirt or some other kind of nonsense. She managed to get to her car and leave, but the incident left Bonnie shaken enough to tell me about it."

"Did anything else happen?"

"No. As far as I know, Owen never bothered her again."

Reed's jaw clenched. "Why didn't you tell me about this earlier?"

Margaret bit her lip. "I'm sorry, Reed. To be honest, it slipped my mind until Will mentioned that Owen might be a suspect. The argument between Bonnie and Owen happened at least six months before she disappeared."

Reed wrestled back his frustration. Cold case investigations often got new information this way. Something that seemed benign long ago suddenly took on new meaning.

"Margaret, do you believe Bonnie ran off?" Emma asked.

She shifted in her soft-soled shoes and hugged herself tighter. "Frankly, I never did."

Reed sucked in a sharp breath. "But...you told me differently."

"I know. I didn't want to get your hopes up if I was wrong. The former sheriff was so certain Bonnie had taken off. He made it seem like I couldn't trust my own insights about my friend. After all, I hadn't known about her relationship with Joshua."

Reed pinched the bridge of his nose and fought back his frustration. The former sheriff had done a lot of damage to the investigation.

"We need to call Austin right now and tell him to stop the search immediately," Emma said. She started for the house. "Don't let them step into the woods on my property."

"What?" Reed chased after her. "Why?"

"Because I have an idea."

Emma refused to explain her plan until Cooper and Austin arrived. Reed wasn't going to like it, and she needed reinforcements. Once they were all settled at the kitchen table, each with a fresh cup of coffee, she displayed an aerial view of her property on a tablet.

"Let's do a quick review of what we know," she said. "I inherit my uncle's property and move to Heyworth. Shortly thereafter, someone starts breaking things on my property and making scary phone calls telling me to leave town. Then poisoned meat is left out for Sadie to eat. As a result, I file a police report. A week goes by and nothing else happens on the property. We now know that's because my stalker was looking for and arranging to hire Charlie."

She paused and Cooper nodded for her to go on.

"Charlie breaks into my house and attacks me," Emma continued. "Subsequently, Reed launches an investigation. Charlie is instructed to get rid of me and Reed. He calls in reinforcements—his brother, Mike, and his cousin, Vernon. They hatch a scheme to kidnap Vernon's daughter while she's on a camping trip with her mother and stepfather. As the nearest SAR team, it's almost guaranteed Sadie and I will be called out to aid in the search. The basic idea is to kill us once we locate Molly, but Vernon has poor aim and—based on the conversation Austin overheard Vernon having—probably didn't want to be responsible for the actual murders. He calls one of his cousins, most likely Charlie, and tells him to hurry up and get there so he can finish the job."

"Fortunately for us, he was late," Austin muttered.

"Agreed. When the attack falls apart and Vernon is arrested, a new plan is made. Charlie and Mike storm the hospital to rescue their cousin and kill me. Two of the hired hitmen are killed in the process—Vernon and Charlie—but Mike escapes. That's what we know and what we can prove."

"Right." Cooper drained the last of his coffee.

"The ultimate question is why would anyone want to kill both Reed and I?" Emma rose from her chair and grabbed the carafe of coffee, refilling each man's cup before her own. "Reed believes his sister's disappearance may have something to do with it. Cooper, you think someone—probably my cousin Owen—has hidden something on the property he doesn't want us to uncover." She took a deep breath. "I think you both may be right."

Reed's eyes widened as he followed her chain of thought. Austin, midsip of his coffee, choked and started coughing.

Cooper frowned. "What are you suggesting? That Bonnie's body is somewhere on your property?"

"No, that Bonnie is alive and being held captive somewhere on my property."

All of the men stared at her in disbelief. Emma pointed to the tablet, showing the aerial view of her property. "I have large swatches of wooded areas on my land. That was perfect for me because I intended to use it as a training area for the canines, but it also means it would be easy for someone to slip on and off the property without me knowing."

"Hold on, hold on." Cooper put up a hand. "If Bonnie was alive on your property, then wouldn't you have found her by now? I mean the kidnapper has to keep her in some kind of structure."

"But it could be an underground bunker. There have been cases like that."

"Even if that's true, the kidnapper would just move Bonnie."

"But he couldn't get rid of the structure," Emma said. "Bonnie's scent would linger long enough the dogs might pick up on it. Or improvements to the land could uncover the bunker. DNA, fingerprints… It would be nearly impossible to get rid of all the evidence inside, right? Especially if Bonnie has been there for a long time."

Cooper nodded slowly. "That's true. It would be hard to clean away all the evidence."

"Which leaves the kidnapper at risk. Plus, he would have to arrange for a new hiding place for Bonnie. It would be far easier to keep her where she is and gain control of the property. Owen has been desperate to get his hands on this land from day one."

Reed inhaled sharply. His gaze dropped to the map before rising to meet hers. "Margaret said Owen was angry with Bonnie for refusing to go out with him."

Emma nodded. "Owen's interactions with me prove he holds on to grudges. Bonnie and Owen went to high school together. Who knows how long he's been interested in her."

"And interest can turn to obsession."

She snapped her fingers. "Like that."

Emma could've kicked herself for not putting two and two together faster. The conversation with Margaret was the missing link they needed.

Cooper's gaze jumped back and forth between her and Reed. "That's a lot of conjecture."

"But it makes sense," Emma continued. "Sadie is an air-scenting dog as opposed to a tracking dog. A tracking dog takes a specific person's scent and follows it to locate only that person. Sadie, however, will find any person lost in a given area. So, let's say I'm running a training exercise and I sent someone into my woods to be the lost person—" she put air quotes around lost person "—Sadie is sent into the woods to find the person. She doesn't know which specific person I'm looking for. She just knows to find someone."

"She could stumble across Bonnie by accident," Reed finished.

"Exactly. That's why I told you to stop the search and not let anyone in the woods on my property. I need to split the acres into sizable chunks and have Sadie search them. My hope is she'll find Bonnie."

"Absolutely not." Reed sliced a hand through the air. "It's too dangerous. Mike is still on the loose. We'll get another team to do the search."

She opened her mouth to object, but Cooper cut her off. "There is no other team available. We've got several missing hikers two counties over. They're aiding in that search."

"So ask one team to come here."

"Based on what, Reed?" Cooper asked. "A theory? Right now, we have no physical evidence indicating Bonnie is anywhere near here. Those missing hikers are a certainty and their lives are on the line."

"He's right," Emma said. She crossed her arms over her chest and reminded herself to stay calm. She couldn't be angry with Reed for wanting to protect her. The last few days had been harrowing. At the same time, if she was right, time was of the essence. There was no way to know what kind of rations Bonnie had. She wouldn't survive long without food or water. "Sadie and I are available, and we can do it."

"What if we do a thorough foot search?" Reed asked. "We've got enough law enforcement."

"There's nothing better for these kinds of searches than a canine. Sadie can cover a larger area faster and her nose won't miss Bonnie, even if she's hidden underground."

"There are things we can do to lessen the risk." Austin pointed at the map. "We can set up patrols along the main road and assign deputies and troopers to keep an eye on the back roads, too. If there's a clear law enforcement presence, it should dissuade Mike from attempting anything."

"*Should* is the operative word in that sentence," Reed argued. "There's no guarantee."

"I'm willing to accept the risk." Emma jutted up her chin. "This is my job, and I'm going to do it."

Reed sighed and his shoulders dropped. "Fine. You win." He met her gaze. "But I'm going with you and Sadie. You have your job, and I have mine. I have every intention of keeping you safe during the search."

TWELVE

By noon, the coolness of the morning had morphed into a warm spring day. Reed rested on a rock under the shade of an oak tree. The radio on his hip crackled and various voices and codes filtered out. Shifts were changing among the deputies and troopers assigned around the property.

Sadie had cleared almost half of the wooded acreage. There was no sign of Bonnie.

Emma threw a ball, and Sadie streaked after it. Reed's gaze scanned the field, lake and tree line. Nothing moved. He was probably being overly cautious. After all, Sadie was likely to be the first one to let them know if a stranger was nearby. He reached inside his backpack and pulled out a bottle of water.

"Let's take a break for lunch." Emma dropped down next to him. Her cheeks were flushed with exertion, and the color brought out the gold flecks in her eyes. "Sadie needs a rest."

The dog joined them. She collapsed in the grass, panting, her fur shining in the sunlight.

"It looks like she's smiling," Reed remarked.

Emma laughed, pulling a small cooler out of her backpack. "She is. Sadie loves to work. The playtime afterward doesn't hurt."

Reed's cell phone beeped, and he checked the message. "I got an email from your uncle's attorney, Emma. Owen wouldn't have received any money under Jeb's will unless he'd been sober for a year. But there's another trust."

Her forehead wrinkled as she waved a hand to shoo away a fly. "From Aunt Rachel?"

"Yep. Apparently, she inherited some money from her parents and set it aside for Owen. He gained access to it when he turned thirty-five. His birthday was four days before Charlie was hired."

"Well, I guess that explains where he got the money." She took a long drink of water, her gaze drifting over the field. In the distance, the lake sparkled in the sunlight. "You know Owen taught me to fish right over there."

"I remember. I'm sorry, Emma."

She let out a breath and tilted her head. "I'm not the only one with a connection to this place. Bonnie loved to fish here, too."

"Yes, she did. Bonnie convinced Judge Norton to let us cut through his property from ours to get here."

The large clearing and the lake sat on the border of intersecting properties. Joshua was to the north and Judge Norton was to the east. Jeb's land extended to the south and west. Back when Reed was a teenager, everything bordering Jeb's land had belonged to the judge.

Emma removed her sandwich from the plastic bag. "Cookies."

"What?"

"Bonnie used my grandmother's recipe and baked Judge Norton a batch of chocolate chip cookies. Judge Norton was hooked on them. He agreed to let her cut across the property, as long as she would keep baking them for him."

Reed laughed. "I should've known he wrangled some kind of bargain out of it."

"Judge Norton's the one who inspired Bonnie to become a paralegal, isn't he?"

"Yes, he did. But her ultimate dream was to be an attorney."

Bonnie had been working and saving money for law school. Her bank account had a hefty sum of cash in it. She'd been halfway to her dream before she disappeared.

Emma let out a long breath. "I'm sorry, Reed. I shouldn't have brought it up."

"No." He glanced at the lake again. "Actually, it's nice to remember the good times. I spend so much of my time thinking about her case. But that's not Bonnie, you know?"

His sister was warm and loving, quick to laugh and always there to help a friend. Reed had a mountain of childhood memories about her he never discussed.

"Yeah, I know what you mean." Emma met his gaze, understanding etched in the curve of her brow and the tilt of her lips. "Bonnie is so much more than the moment of her disappearance."

His breath caught. He'd forgotten how easily Emma saw straight into his heart. Reed dropped his gaze under the pretense of grabbing a banana from his lunch sack. Their near kiss in the hospital lingered in his mind, but he did his best to snuff out the memory. They'd agreed to be friends and Emma had been under a lot of stress. It wouldn't be smart to assume one small moment between them meant anything.

"Is it hard being in Heyworth?" she asked. "You always talked about never coming back. Returning under these circumstances can't be easy."

"Well, I did return because Bonnie disappeared, but I was already making plans to move home anyway."

"You were?"

He nodded. "My mom's depression was hard on me. I didn't understand it and I spent a lot of time angry with her. When she didn't get out of bed for weeks, taking care of Bonnie fell on my shoulders. Making the meals, getting ready for school, all of it. I wanted to escape and never look back."

Remembering his immaturity and lack of compassion shamed him. His mother had been struggling. Reed knew that now.

"College opened my eyes a bit," he continued. "I found a deeper connection with the Lord. Then I joined the Austin police academy. Living in a big city set me straight. Yes, my mom's depression created obstacles in my life, but I still had family—Aunt Bessie and Uncle Ray—plus the whole town. Neighbors would bring casseroles and cheer me on at track meets. Your uncle gave me work. Jeb paid far more than he should have so I could make the bills. That kind of community doesn't happen everywhere and there a lot of kids out there who never get to experience it."

Emma sighed. "Like me."

"Yeah. I remembered everything you said, and I started to look at things very differently. I wanted to give back to Heyworth. I applied to work in the sheriff's department and was on the waiting list to become a deputy. Then Bonnie disappeared. Everything changed. The sheriff wasn't as careful with cases as he should've been. I set out to run against him and won the election."

Her lips turned up into a beautiful smile. "Heyworth is fortunate to have you."

"It's home. It took me a long time to realize it, but I'm glad I did. My mom and I healed our relationship before she passed away, too." He blinked at the sudden rush of emotions washing over him. "I'm very grateful for that."

"So am I."

She shifted and leaned her head against his shoulder. Reed took her hand, interlacing their fingers together. The wind ruffled his hair, and for a brief moment, he allowed himself to simply be present with her.

Something moving across the field caught his attention. He frowned. "What's Sadie doing?"

The dog was sniffing around a small shack that used to contain fishing tackle.

"She's exploring." Emma sat up and squinted. "Although I think something in the shack has caught her attention. There's not much in there, aside from Jeb's fishing gear and some tools. I padlocked it once stuff started happening around the property."

He stood. "Do you have the key on you?"

"Yep. I grabbed it when I knew we would be doing a search of the property." She opened a zipper on her backpack and pulled out a ring of keys. "Reed, Bonnie can't be in there. I've checked it out already."

"Still worth taking a look at what has Sadie's interest." Reed scanned the tree line again. Everything was clear. He stepped out of the shadows and into the sunlight. "Stay with me."

They crossed the field. As they drew closer to the shack, the wind shifted. A rotten smell drifted over them. Emma gagged. "Oh, no."

Reed's gut twisted. He'd know that scent anywhere.

It was decomposition.

He paused at the shack door. The lock was closed and appeared undamaged. Still, he pulled a set of gloves out of his pocket and put them on. "Stay outside, Emma. And keep Sadie back, too."

She ordered the dog to sit and Sadie promptly did. Reed twisted the key in the lock. The door swung open and the smell become overpowering. He made a conscious effort to breathe through his mouth.

The inside of the shack was dim. A small table covered in fishing lures sat on one side. Poles and nets were stacked against the far wall. The only light came from the open doorway.

Reed's boots made no sound against the cement as he edged farther inside. He blinked, giving his eyes time to adjust. A clump of fur in the corner caught his attention. The knot in his stomach loosened.

"It's clear." He grimaced. "It's a raccoon."

Emma appeared in the doorway, Sadie by her side. "Oh, no. Maybe I locked the poor thing in."

He turned, his gaze sweeping the shack. Emma moved and the sunlight shifted. Something winked on the cement floor. Reed bent down. With a gloved hand, he reached under the table and pulled out a bracelet.

"What is it?" Emma edged closer. She had a hand over her nose. "Where did that come from?"

Reed couldn't look away. The silver infinity band was dusty, but the diamond cross in the center still held some of its shine. His hand trembled.

"Reed? Are you okay?"

He blinked at Emma. His mouth opened, but he couldn't quite form the words on his lips. "This…this… It's my sister's bracelet. This belongs to Bonnie."

Sadie growled.

The distinctive sound of a shotgun being pumped cut it off.

Before Emma could blink, Reed positioned himself between her and the doorway. He pulled his weapon. She gave a hand signal to Sadie to keep her quiet. The scent inside the shed turned her stomach but was far less terrifying than the unknown individual outside with a shotgun.

"You there in the shed," a man bellowed. "I've got my weapon pointed right at ya. Come out with your hands up."

Emma let out the breath she was holding. She stood up on her tiptoes to whisper in Reed's ear. "It's Wayne Johnson."

Wayne was a jack-of-all-trades. He was hired by many of the farms and ranches when they needed an extra hand. She'd recently employed him herself.

Reed's stance relaxed. "Wayne, it's Sheriff Atkinson and Emma Pierce."

"Sheriff?" Wayne's voice wobbled. If Emma's heart wasn't still racing from fear, she would've felt sorry for the man. No doubt the last thing he wanted to do was pull a weapon on a lawman.

"Put your shotgun on the ground and step away from it," Reed ordered.

"Yes, sir."

There was movement outside the shed. Reed held a hand up, indicating Emma should stay behind him. They edged to the doorway.

Wayne came into view. Midsixties and toothpick lean, he was dressed in faded overalls and a straw hat. A tool belt hung from his narrow hips. Wayne's shotgun rested in the grass several yards away.

Reed lowered his weapon and holstered it. Emma came around from behind him, taking her first deep breath of clean air. It took two more to clear the scent of the dead raccoon from her nose.

Wayne shifted in his worn boots. "I'm really sorry, Sheriff. I didn't know it was y'all in there. I've heard around town that Emma's been having some problems on the property. When I saw the shed was open, I figured there might be trouble." His gaze drifted to Emma. "Sorry to frighten you, ma'am."

"That's quite all right, Wayne." She mustered up a re-assuring smile. "I appreciate you keeping an eye out."

"Where did you come from?" Reed asked.

Wayne waved a gnarled hand toward the far side of the clearing. "I was doing some fence repairs for Judge Norton."

"Why are you carrying a shotgun?"

"Cuz of all the stuff happening on Emma's land. Folks ain't sure who's behind it, and I'm working on a remote part of the ranch. Don't want to get caught off guard."

His explanation made sense, and in Texas, it was legal to openly carry a firearm. Wayne hadn't done anything wrong.

"Excuse me a moment." Reed jogged over to the tree line where they'd had lunch and retrieved an evidence bag. He dropped Bonnie's bracelet inside.

Emma glanced at the shed. A thousand questions ran through her mind. If Bonnie had been wearing the brace-let on the day she disappeared, then logic dictated she'd been on the property. "Wayne, you do a lot of work for Judge Norton, right?"

Wayne nodded. "From time to time when he needs me."

"Have you ever heard anything strange while in this area? Or seen something that didn't sit right with you?"

Reed returned, catching the tail end of her question. Wayne shifted in his boots again and tugged on his tool belt. "Whatta ya mean by strange?"

Right. She should be more specific. "Have you seen a woman on the property?"

Another long pause. His forehead wrinkled. "Only you and the lady you live with."

"Have you ever heard a woman crying or calling for help in this area?"

He squinted at her, probably because the question was an odd one. Wayne shook his head. "No, ma'am. If I'd heard somethin' like that, I would've told ya."

Emma chewed on the inside of her cheek. It'd been a long shot, but worth trying. She decided to change tactics. "Have you seen Owen coming and going from the property since I moved here?"

There was another long pause. Wayne rubbed the back of his neck. "Listen, I don't wanna get anyone in trouble—"

"This is a police investigation," Reed interrupted. "If you know something, you need to tell me."

"I did see him the other day talkin' to Joshua. Actually, they weren't so much talkin' as they were arguin'."

"What day was this?"

"Uhhh, musta been on Tuesday. That's the day I was doing a check on the fences to see which ones needed work. I heard some yellin' and came to check it out. When I saw it was just Owen and Joshua, I left."

Emma passed a glance to Reed. The argument happened on the same day Owen had attacked Emma on her porch.

"Did you hear what they were arguing about?" Reed asked.

"No, but it seemed pretty heated from what I saw. Owen was makin' a big old ruckus. You know that boy has a fiery temper, especially when he's had a few beers."

"Have you seen him around the property any other time?"

"Naw, just that once." Wayne adjusted his tool belt. "If y'all don't mind, I'd better get back to mendin' the fences."

"Sure, but if you think of anything else, give me a call."

"Will do, Sheriff." Wayne tipped his hat toward Emma before collecting his shotgun and ambling back to the property line.

Emma waited until he was out of hearing range. "I don't get it. None of this is making any sense. It's like one of those jigsaw puzzles you liked to do. I have a piece here and a piece there, but getting the whole picture is impossible. How did Bonnie's bracelet get inside the shed? And what does Owen and Joshua's fight have to do with anything?"

"One may have nothing to do with the other. Owen and Joshua used to run in the same crowd. The argument could be about any number of things."

"Okay." Emma took a deep breath. "Then we'll deal with just the bracelet. Is it possible Bonnie lost it in there before she went missing?"

"I don't think so. This bracelet originally belonged to my mother. Bonnie never took it off. I think it's safe to assume she was wearing it the day she disappeared."

"Then she was held in the shed."

"Yes, but there's no indication someone has been held there for an extended period of time."

"So Bonnie was there, but only for a short while. Long enough to lose her bracelet."

Reed's gaze went from the shed to the lake. His jaw tightened. "There may be another explanation for why we can't find Bonnie, her car or her suitcase."

The water sparkled in the sunlight, but a cold finger of dread coursed down Emma's spine as she followed his logic.

Everything they were looking for could be underwater.

THIRTEEN

The next several days melded into each other. Reed's emotions vacillated between relief, frustration and a renewed sense of urgency. The lake was dredged, but nothing more sinister than an old kitchen sink lay at the bottom. Emma's property was thoroughly searched—first by her and Sadie, then by cadaver dogs and law enforcement. Nothing new was uncovered.

Cases went like this. Reed had been in law enforcement long enough to know it was sometimes three steps forward and two back. Still, it was hard to be patient.

The front door to his house opened, and Emma stepped onto the porch. His breath hitched in his throat. She'd traded her normal jeans and T-shirt for a beautiful sundress. It swirled around her shapely legs and brought out the red highlights in her hair.

"Sorry," she said breathlessly. "It's so warm out, I almost forgot my sweater. The air-conditioning can be a bit cold."

"No worries. Church service doesn't start for another forty-five minutes. We have plenty of time."

He held open the passenger side door to the SUV. Emma breezed by him, the scent of vanilla lingering even after she'd lifted herself into the seat. Reed's hand tightened on the handle. Days of being together were adding up. Dinners at Aunt Bessie's with Vivian and Lily, time spent searching Emma's property, hours spent poring over every police report in Bonnie's case.

Each moment had deepened Reed's feelings for Emma, and it was becoming increasingly harder to ignore them.

"Thanks for arranging this," Emma said, once they were on the road. "Church sets my whole week up right. I don't feel the same when I miss it."

"I know. It's important to me, too." Reed had debated the risk until this morning. Mike, it seemed, had gone underground. There hadn't been any additional threats toward Emma. While Reed wasn't convinced things were over, he felt comfortable enough to attend Sunday morning service.

Emma cast a glance at him from the corner of her eye. "You've changed. You always attended church, but it seems your faith has grown deeper."

"I've gotten some bumps and bruises along the way. Hard times can push you toward your faith, if you let it."

"I know what you mean. When Mark died, I was lost." She smoothed a hand down her skirt. "He never even knew I was pregnant. I didn't get the chance to tell him."

"Ah, Em. I'm so sorry."

"I was heartbroken and terrified. In an instant, I became a widow with a baby on the way. I'd just graduated from vet school but didn't have job. We were living on a military base, so I had to move. Prayer helped pull me through."

"Where did you go after you moved off base?"

"To live with Vivi. She had her own grief—Mark was her only sibling—and we didn't know each other well, but Vivian jumped right in to help out. She changed her whole life for us."

His respect for Emma's sister-in-law deepened. The

choices Vivian had made weren't easy, and he'd seen lots of families that didn't weather the storm together. "I'm glad you had her."

"Me, too. She even supported the move to Heyworth. Vivian understood the need for community and family. I want Lily to have connections she can rely on for her whole life. Church is a big part of it, too."

"There's something special about worshiping together."

"Yes." She smiled, her entire face lighting up. "Exactly."

The church was cool when they stepped inside. Aunt Bessie caught sight of them and waved. Vivian was holding Lily. The little girl bounced on her aunt's hip and squealed for joy when she spotted her mom.

Emma scooped her up into her arms, planting several kisses on her face. "Good morning, baby girl."

Reed kissed his aunt's cheek and greeted Vivian. Austin said in a low voice, "No one followed us here. Deputy Irving reported everything has been quiet at Emma's house, as well. I suspect Mike is sitting on a beach in Mexico somewhere."

"Could be. Still, we don't know who hired him." Owen was still missing, and they hadn't been able to link either him or Joshua to any of the hitmen. "If the person stalking Emma was willing to hire someone once, there's no saying he won't do it again. We have to stay vigilant."

Austin nodded. His gaze flickered to Vivian before returning to Reed. "Agreed."

They all settled into their seats. Lily crawled over to Reed's lap halfway through the service and flashed him an adorable smile. He planted a kiss on her sweet head. Having Emma at his side and Lily in his arms was a double whammy on his heart. The intervening days had been stressful and emotionally draining, but spending time with them renewed him in a way he hadn't thought was possible.

Reed had closed himself off from the possibility of having a wife and children because being sheriff required all of his energy. He never wanted another family to go through what he had with Bonnie. What he hadn't considered, until now, was that having Emma and Lily in his life actually made him better at his job. Like prayer and attending church service, their presence and affection centered him.

After the final hymn, parishioners beelined in small groups to the fellowship room for coffee and donuts. Aunt Bessie picked up her purse from the chair and slung it over her shoulder. "Service was lovely, wasn't it?"

"It was." Vivian brushed a slim hand through her honey-colored locks. "I wish we could stay for the fellowship."

A twinge of guilt prickled Reed. Vivian had been trapped at Aunt Bessie's house for days. A crease formed between Emma's brows and he knew she was thinking the same thing. They were surrounded by half of the town and escorted by two law enforcement officers. It would safe enough.

"Ten minutes of fellowship can't hurt," he said. Reed spotted Harry Norton standing off to the side. The tall, slender widower was chatting with the mayor and his wife. Will was with them, too. "Austin, do you mind keeping an eye out for them? I want to talk to Judge Norton."

"Sure thing."

Emma handed Lily to her sister-in-law. "I'll stay with Reed and meet you back at the house."

"Don't be late, dear." Aunt Bessie grinned. "I have homemade cinnamon rolls rising as we speak. Once we get home, I'll pop them in the oven."

"Is there cream cheese frosting involved?" Emma asked.

Aunt Bessie winked. "Of course."

Reed chuckled. "Then we'll definitely be on time. Otherwise, Austin will eat them all."

His cousin shot him a mock glare. "I take offense to that. Last time you were thirty minutes late. What's a man to do?"

The whole group laughed. They separated, but the judge was still speaking with the mayor. Reed caught Will's eye and the prosecutor nodded discreetly. Reed and Emma hung back to wait for a chance to speak to Harry.

"Do you really think it's possible Joshua and Owen are working together?" she asked Reed quietly.

"At this point, I'm checking out every avenue. The argument between the two men could be nothing, but since we didn't find anything else on your property, it puts Joshua higher on my suspect list. Maybe he's involved. Or maybe he knows something but won't tell us."

"Why not question Joshua about the fight?"

"I don't want to tip him off that I know about it yet. It's better to gather as much information as I can."

Emma's gaze drifted back to Will and Judge Norton. "Joshua wasn't the only man Bonnie dated. Will was a former boyfriend. Have you considered him as a suspect?"

"Early on I did, but Will was very cooperative. He allowed me to search his home, answered all my questions, and the information he gave me checked out. Plus, he has an alibi for the time of my sister's disappearance. At least, he sort of does. He ran a red light on Main Street, and the camera caught it. He got an automatic ticket. The timing made it impossible for Will to be on Main Street and in Franklin Park where Bonnie disappeared from at the same time."

Emma jerked her chin. "They're done and coming this way."

* * *

Emma's nerves jittered as she watched Will and his uncle approach. Side by side, the two men shared a striking resemblance. They had the same stature, the same patrician nose. Judge Norton's silver hair was slicked back from his face, drawing attention to his striking eyes and high forehead. Now in his late sixties, Harry had worked as a county judge for the last twenty years after a successful career as a prosecutor. There wasn't a person in town he didn't know.

"Sheriff, it's good to see you." Harry shook Reed's hand, his dark brown eyes crinkling at the corners.

"You, too, sir. Allow me to introduce Emma Pierce."

"Ms. Pierce, it's lovely to meet you." The judge shook her hand, as well. His grip was firm but not bruising. The slight smile dropped from his lips and his expression turned grave. "I'm so sorry to hear about the trouble you've been having."

"Thank you, sir."

Harry clapped Will on the back. "My nephew says you're building a canine SAR training facility."

Emma nodded. "It's a big project, but I'm excited about the opportunity."

"I'm so pleased. Your uncle was a cherished member of our community and I know he'd be proud to have his land used in such an important manner."

It wasn't the first time she'd heard the sentiment. Several members of Heyworth had told her the same. Still, it never failed to reinforce her decision. Honoring her uncle's wishes was a blessing she gratefully accepted.

"Judge Norton, I'd like to ask you a few questions about the land sale you made to Joshua Lowe last year," Reed said.

The older man's brow wrinkled. "What about it?"

"As I remember, that piece of property wasn't for sale at the time. What made you sell it?"

"Joshua came to my office and specifically asked for it." Emma rocked back on her heels. "He did?"

"Well, it's not a surprise." Harry ran a hand down his tie in a gesture very similar to his nephew's classic move. "Joshua had saved up some money. He was looking to get a fresh start in life. I was under the impression he'd tried to buy from some others in the county, but they'd refused to sell on account of his reputation. I, however, had grown to know and like Joshua over the years."

Harry's reasoning wasn't a shock. Uncle Jeb had spoken highly of Judge Norton to Emma many times. The two men had liked and respected each other. Judge Norton believed strongly in the power of redemption. He often encouraged those who appeared in front of his bench to improve their lives.

Will rolled his eyes. Clearly, he didn't share his uncle's opinion.

"Joshua figured I would be willing to give him a helping hand," Judge Norton continued. "That particular section of my land had the old foreman house on it, so it was a logical choice."

"When did he first contact you to purchase it?" Reed asked.

"Hmm, I would say about a week before we finalized the deal."

Will's gaze narrowed. "So he asked to purchase the property a week before Bonnie disappeared, and the actual sale went through the day before she supposedly left town. That's interesting."

Judge Norton frowned. "I don't think I like your tone or what you're implying."

Will's cheeks heated at the reprimand. "You sold that

property to a criminal. I know you like to think of Joshua as your pet project, but a leopard doesn't change its spots."

"Will, I know you had feelings for Bonnie—"

"Don't you dare, Uncle Harry." The color spread to the tops of his ears. "It wasn't a fleeting relationship. I cared deeply about her."

Emma blinked, her gaze shifting back and forth between the two men. She'd known Bonnie and Will had dated, but she hadn't realized they were serious. From the way Reed's brows drew down, the news was a surprise to him, as well.

"Why did the two of you break up?" Emma asked.

"I was stupid." Will pressed two fingers against the bridge of his nose. "A long-distance relationship seemed too hard, and I didn't want to hold her back from law school. But breaking up was a terrible mistake. I thought I was setting Bonnie free to pursue her dreams. Instead, I hurt her. If I hadn't broken up with Bonnie, she never would've started dating Joshua."

Guilt laced every word. It seemed Reed wasn't the only one carrying around a boatload of regrets. Will dropped his hand. Tears shimmered in his eyes. "Excuse me. I think I need some fresh air."

He marched out.

Judge Norton watched his nephew go and gave a deep sigh, before turning back to Reed. "Sheriff, I genuinely don't believe Joshua had anything to do with Bonnie's disappearance. Maybe you'll chalk me up as being an optimistic fool, but I'm proud of Joshua. He had a rough time growing up. His father was a horrible man with a long criminal record. His mother was strung out on drugs much of the time. All he needed was someone to believe in him. When I offered Joshua the option to go into a work program instead of jail, he took it. They told me he was one of the hardest working ranch hands they'd ever seen. Two years later, he had saved up enough to purchase the land from me."

Joshua's apparent turnaround didn't mean he couldn't have hurt Bonnie. Sometimes things happened in the heat of the moment. Although, Emma could see Judge Norton's point. There was nothing in Joshua's criminal record to indicate he was violent, and he'd stayed out of trouble for years.

"Your opinion means a lot to me, Judge," Reed said. "I'll keep it in mind."

They said their goodbyes. Reed placed a hand on the small of Emma's back as they left the church and walked across the parking lot. Her gaze swept across the vehicles. Sunshine bounced off the windshields, making it impossible to see inside them.

"Well, Judge Norton muddied the waters." Emma bit her lip. "What do you think?"

"I'm not sure…" His voice trailed off. He pulled Emma closer. "I think someone's watching us."

She stiffened. Reed scanned the lot. Nothing moved, but a knot in Emma's stomach tightened. Was Mike close by? Reed wasn't one to create drama, and she trusted his instincts.

Reed picked up the pace, hitting the fob on his SUV. He ushered Emma inside and closed the door. They pulled out of the church parking lot onto Main Street. Traffic was light at this hour. Emma kept alert, watching the street for any potential danger, but nothing seemed out of the ordinary.

Suddenly, a beat-up Ford shot out of the parking lot of a local fast-food restaurant. Mud obscured the license plates. Emma's heart jumped into her throat. The truck was heading straight for them, and she tensed for impact.

Reed swerved. The truck narrowly missed sideswiping

them. It clipped the bumper before tearing off down the street. Through the roar in her ears, Emma heard Reed calling for backup.

"It was Mike," she said. For one brief moment, right before Reed swerved, she'd been face-to-face with the driver.

With the man who wanted to kill her.

FOURTEEN

Emma sighed. The bed was comfortable and the house was quiet, but she couldn't sleep. The ceiling fan whirled above her, running at the same speed as her thoughts. How long could they keep going like this? Spending time with Lily in short bursts did nothing to ease the ache in her heart. She missed her little girl more and more every day.

At the same time, Mike was still out there. Not to mention the man who'd hired him. Despite everyone's best efforts, they were no closer to solving the case than they had been a few days ago. They still weren't entirely sure why Emma was a target in the first place.

Lord, I know You're guiding me, but I don't know where to. This is so hard.

The prayer gave her a measure of comfort. Fluffing her pillow, Emma rolled over and snuggled into the soft bedding.

Sleep eluded her. She tossed off the comforter. Sadie raised her head from her place at the foot of the bed.

"Stay here, girl." Emma ran a hand over her soft fur. "I'll go get some tea."

Emma eased out of the bedroom. Austin's door was open, his bed unmade. He'd gone to headquarters to work after lunch at Aunt Bessie's. Chances were he was still there.

The light in the kitchen was on. She rounded the corner to find Reed sitting at the table. His hair was mussed, as if his fingers had run through it dozens of times, and bristles darkened his strong jaw. A laptop was perched at his elbow. The table's surface was covered with papers.

He glanced up. In all the time she'd known him, Reed had never appeared tired. Until now. Shadows rested under his gorgeous eyes, and the faint lines around his mouth had deepened. Emma mentally berated herself. She'd spent her time worrying about how this was affecting her, but what about Reed? This had to be torturous for him.

"Are you okay?" he asked.

"I couldn't sleep and thought some tea might help. Would you like some?"

"That's a good idea. I need something other than all the coffee I've had today. By the way, deputies located the truck Mike used to nearly run us off the road. It'd been reported stolen earlier in the day."

Another dead end. Emma grabbed the electric kettle and filled it with water. "What are you working on?"

"I'm trying to find some connection between Owen and the hitmen or Joshua and the hitmen. There's nothing though. They haven't been in jail together. They didn't go to the same school or frequent the same places. We interviewed friends and family, not that it helped a lot. No one seems to know much of anything."

"Maybe neither of them are involved. We could be moving in the wrong direction."

He rubbed his eyes. "I know, but my gut says otherwise. There has to be something I'm missing."

"The local bar seems like a place all of them would hang out."

"I thought the same, but Charlie and Mike liked to hang with their cousin Vernon for the most part. They always went over to the next town."

Emma poured hot water into two mugs and left the tea to steep on the counter. She took a closer look at the papers. There were printouts of criminal records. One caught her eye.

"Joshua looks so young here." His cheeks were plump, his skin mottled with acne. "How old was he when he started getting into trouble?"

"Twelve. His juvie record is spotty. That photograph was taken when he was seventeen. He'd been arrested for breaking and entering. Stole some electronic equipment from a home while the owners were on vacation."

She scanned his criminal record. "Looks like he had a habit of breaking into houses. It's a shame Joshua didn't have parents who taught him the right path…" Her voice trailed off and she stiffened. "Reed, what if you're look-ing at the wrong Lowe?"

"What do you mean?"

"Joshua's father was a criminal. Maybe he and one of the Young brothers crossed paths a long time ago."

His fingers flew over the keyboard. Moments later, he gave an excited yelp. "That's it! I can't believe I missed this. Joshua's dad and Charlie Young were arrested for a string of robberies in nearby Glatten. We never went back into Joshua's childhood. If we interview neighbors, we might be able to prove Joshua knew Charlie and maybe even Mike. It's a tenuous link, but it's a place to start."

Reed got up from the chair and hugged her. "You're a genius."

"I don't know about genius, but I'll take the compli-ment all the same." She laughed and pulled back slightly. "I'm glad I could help."

"You do help. More than you realize."

Reed's gaze dropped to her mouth. He hesitated and she could see the questions in his eyes. In an instant, Emma realized Vivian had been right. Reed was holding back, not because he didn't want this, but because he wasn't sure about her feelings.

"I haven't dated since Mark died." The words burst from her like a dam cracked open. "My goal was to start fresh in Heyworth. To start Helping Paws and raise Lily. Everything is a mess right now because of the case." She didn't want to think about what would happen if they didn't find the person after her. One thing at a time. Emma took a deep breath. "And I don't know if I have it in me to fall in love again. Especially given your job. I know that's not fair, but losing Mark was awful. I don't want to go through it again."

He lifted a hand to cup her face and butterflies erupted in her stomach. "Emma…"

"At the same time, I care about you, Reed. Beyond just friendship. And I don't know what to do about it."

"That makes two of us. I don't know what the future holds, Em, but I'm thankful to have this moment with you."

Reed bent his head and kissed her. The warmth of his touch spread through her like molten lava. She lost herself in it. Everything about this man called to her. His bravery, his honesty, his goodness. In Reed's arms, she was protected and cared for. Nothing else existed except for the feel of his lips against hers, the gentle caress of his hand on her face, and the feelings they shared.

Reed's phone rang. He broke the kiss. "Sorry, Em. I have to grab that. It could be headquarters."

He scooped up the phone from the table and answered.

"Sheriff, there's been an explosion on Emma's property." Deputy Irving's tone was rushed and loud enough Emma could hear every word. "I've called for backup and the fire department—"

His voice cut off as a boom echoed over the speaker.

"Deputy Irving," Reed yelled into the phone. "Jack, answer me!"

Silence followed. He checked his phone to ensure the line was still open, but they'd been cut off. His fingers shook slightly as he dialed his deputy's number. *Lord, please. The man has a wife and children.* The phone rang and rang, but Jack didn't answer.

Reed called into Dispatch. "Mona, we may have an officer down. Send every available patrol to Emma's property. Deputy Irving isn't answering my phone call. Radio him now."

"Hold on, sir."

Reed paced the length of the kitchen. For days Emma's property had been crawling with law enforcement due to the search for Bonnie. Tonight was the first time only one deputy was left standing guard. Jack had specifically said there was an explosion and it sounded like there'd been another one right before they'd been cut off.

Mike must be following up his attempt to run them off the road with a new attack.

"I can't get him on the radio," Mona said. Her voice shook. "Backup is on the way, but the closest unit is at least twenty minutes out. Austin was working here at headquarters and he's also heading your direction."

Reed's hand tightened on the phone. He was trying to cover as many people as possible with the staff he had, plus keeping a lookout for Mike and Owen. It was a lot of ground to cover and not enough manpower to do it. "Radio the other units and tell them to approach with extreme caution. If this is Mike, he's probably armed and dangerous. He also has knowledge of explosives."

He hung up. Emma grabbed his sleeve. "We're the closest to him. We have to go."

"That might be exactly the reaction Mike is looking for. He's trying to flush you out."

He scraped a hand through his hair. "The safest thing to do is to stay here."

"Or he could be creating a diversion to draw all the officers to my property so he can attack your house. There's no way to read his mind, Reed, and I'm not leaving Deputy Irving out there for the next twenty minutes by himself."

He wrestled with the decision. There wasn't a good choice either way, and Emma was right. Trying to guess Mike's next move was a futile game. If there was a chance to save his deputy, they had to take it. "You need to do exactly as I say."

"Absolutely."

She hollered for Sadie, who came shooting down the hall. Emma snapped on the dog's leash. Reed grabbed his keys. Together, the dog between them, they hustled to the SUV.

Wind scattered pine needles and brought with it the scent of smoke. The tension in Reed's muscles ratcheted up a notch. If he could smell the fire from his property, it was big.

He paused at the SUV long enough to put on a bulletproof vest and fish out a spare. He handed it to Emma. "Put this on."

She nodded. He hit the gas, blasting out of the driveway and onto the back road leading to Emma's property. The SUV bounced over the ruts. He listened to the radio as his team communicated with each other. The closest unit was still twelve minutes out. Far too long.

He rounded a bend in the road and a brilliant glow glimmered beyond the trees. Reed's hands tightened on the steering wheel.

Emma gasped. "That's my canine facility. All of the handlers' houses are on fire."

They weren't just on fire. They'd been destroyed. Reed's anger burned as bright as the flames, but there was no time for it. He needed to stay focused on finding his deputy while keeping Emma safe. "Get down into the wheel well. If Mike starts shooting, I don't want you to be visible."

Emma unbuckled her seat belt and slipped down. Heat from the blaze washed over them. Sweat beaded on his forehead. Reed scanned for his deputy's patrol car.

"Do you see him?" Emma asked.

"No, but he might be parked in front of your house." He hit the gas, taking them farther from the flames. A flash of red and blue lights caught his attention. As he suspected, Jack's patrol car was parked in Emma's driveway. Reed slammed on the brakes and shoved the SUV into Park. He didn't bother to remove the keys from the ignition. "Stay here."

He eased out of his vehicle, using it as cover. A pair of feet stuck out from the back of the patrol car. The driver's side door was open, but the interior light wasn't on. Reed paused, straining to hear any movement. Nothing. If Mike was out there, he wasn't moving.

Reed quickly closed the distance between him and his deputy, running at a crouch. His breath caught. Jack's face was covered in blood. It looked like he'd been pistol-whipped. Reed grabbed Jack's wrist. A pulse thumped against his fingers.

Thank you, Lord.

For the second time in less than two weeks, he was

standing over one of his men nearly killed in the line of duty. No matter what precautions he put in place to protect others, it seemed Mike and whoever had hired him were one step ahead.

A shot split the night air followed by glass shattering. Emma!

No longer worried about staying in a crouch, Reed raced back to his vehicle. Several shots thudded in the dirt at his feet.

That's right, buddy. Leave her alone. Come and get me.

"Emma." He took shelter at the rear of his vehicle. "Emma, answer me."

"I'm okay, Reed. He missed me." Her voice shook. "Deputy Irving?"

"He's alive."

A motorcycle roared to life in the woods. Reed peeked around his SUV and caught sight of a taillight winking in the distance. The passenger side door to the SUV swung open. The window was missing.

"Reed, get in. Hurry!"

He raced up the side and climbed in. Emma was already in the driver's seat. He didn't have time to close the door before she hit the gas pedal. Wind rushed in through the shot-out window.

"Emma, what are you doing?"

"I'm going after him." She leaned into the steering wheel. "It's enough. If we don't stop him now, how many other people is he going to hurt?"

"No, we aren't chasing him."

"I didn't ask you." Her teeth gritted. She turned onto the main road and the SUV picked up speed. "I've had enough."

The motorcycle's taillight appeared in front of them. Emma sped up even more. The man on the bike passed a glance over his shoulder. The headlights illuminated his face for only half a second, but it was enough to confirm his identity. Mike Young.

Reed radioed in their location, relayed the license plate of the motorcycle and ordered units to intervene. A curve appeared in the road. Emma never slowed down. She took it at a high rate of speed, the back of the vehicle fishtailing. She fought for control of the wheel. Mike shot ahead.

"Emma, we need to stop."

She pounded the steering wheel. "He's getting away."

Reed placed a hand on her arm. "It's too dangerous. Think of Lily."

His words had the desired effect. She slowed to a stop. The motorcycle's taillight disappeared.

"My guys are en route. They'll catch him."

He hoped. Still, chasing Mike down with Emma in the vehicle wasn't just dangerous. It was reckless.

She put the SUV in Park.

"You're right. I'm sorry. I just… He destroyed my facility. He attacked Deputy Irving." She stared out the windshield. Reed's heart cracked at the pain in her voice. "He shot at me. He isn't going to stop."

"I know, but we'll find him."

She nodded and turned the vehicle around. "We should go back and give first aid to your deputy. How badly was he hurt?"

"He was knocked out, but I think he's going to be okay."

They rounded the curve of the driveway. A figure appeared in the headlights. Emma screamed and slammed on the brakes.

Deputy Irving staggered toward them. Blood ran down his face from the injury to his head. Reed opened his door. He looped an arm around Jack's waist.

"We need to go," Jack said. Even injured, he propelled

Reed toward the vehicle. "We need to move. Can't find my keys…can't drive."

"Help is on the way. Let's get you to a hospital."

"No…" He shook his head. Blood spattered on Reed's shoulder. "Went inside for phone… Bomb… House."

Reed glanced behind him. The front door to Emma's house was standing open. It took a second to register what his deputy was trying to tell him. His heart rate skyrocketed. He shoved Jack into the back seat of the SUV and slammed the door.

"Out of the driver's seat, Emma! Fast!"

She didn't ask questions. She scrambled to the passenger side. Reed tossed himself in the driver's seat, did a U-turn and hit the gas.

"Get down," he ordered her.

Reed glanced behind him. One breath. Two.

An explosion rocked the vehicle. Heat rushed over them in a wave. From the back seat, Sadie whined. In the rearview mirror, a huge fireball and thick clouds of smoke rose in the air.

FIFTEEN

The next afternoon, Emma surveyed what was left of her home. The porch her uncle had lovingly made was nothing but a pile of broken wood. Bricks had been blown off the foundation and scattered across the yard like discarded Legos. The chimney towered over a sagged-in, blackened roof.

Tears pricked her eyes. There was nothing left to save. The house would have to be demolished and rebuilt from scratch. Her canine training facility was in worse shape. The handlers' homes had burned to the ground. The fire had spread to the obstacle course and it was gone, as well.

Next to her, Reed let out a low sigh. "Emma, I'm so sorry."

"It's not your fault." She closed her eyes and took a deep breath. A pity party wasn't possible now, and no matter how bad things were, they could've been a whole lot worse. "I'm just glad Deputy Irving is okay, and no one was seriously hurt."

According to the bomb squad, the explosion would've likely killed the deputy if Reed and Emma hadn't driven him away in time. As it was, all he had was a concussion. Deputy Irving had already been released from the hospital and was recuperating at home with his family.

Heavy thunderclouds hung on the horizon. Emma hugged herself against the chill in the air. "Has there been any news from Cooper?"

She hoped this latest attack would provide some key piece of information. They had to find Mike. Soon. Before someone else got hurt.

"Not yet. Austin is personally communicating with every law enforcement agency within a hundred-mile radius. We're also putting out a reward for any information about his whereabouts." Reed's jaw tightened. "Part of me regrets telling you to back off following him."

"No, you were right. I was more likely to get us injured than to catch him. Besides, if we hadn't come back to get Deputy Irving…" She didn't want to consider the alternative. Instead she turned and rested her head on Reed's broad chest. The scent of his aftershave—warm and piney—mingled with the fresh smell of his laundry detergent. She breathed it in, letting it erase the stink of the smoke. "You're doing the best you can. We all are."

He wrapped his arms around her. "It doesn't feel like my best is good enough."

"It is." She pulled him closer. "We just have to keep holding on. Keep working hard, keep praying and lean on our faith."

"I will, but I'd love a break in the case, too."

She chuckled. "I think we all would."

Reed's phone rang and he released her to answer it. Cool air rushed in, replacing the warmth of his body, and Emma shivered.

She stared at the rubble. The loss was crippling. This was supposed to be her fresh start, the beginning of a genuine home living in a town of wonderful people and training dogs in Search and Rescue. It was all slipping away.

Sadie lay in the grass, her head on her paws, a mournful look in her eyes. It wasn't the first time her dog seemed to sense Emma's emotions and share them. Emma bent down to stroke her. "It'll be okay, girl. We'll figure it out."

She didn't know how, but they would. One step at a time.

Reed joined them. "That was Cooper. He's got an update for us and asked to meet at headquarters."

"Let's go then."

The drive to town was quick. Emma stared out the window at the buildings on Main Street. Several ladies sat outside the Clip 'n' Curl with rollers and tinfoil in their hair. The diner was packed for lunch and two men loaded hay into the back of a pickup at the feedstore. Children ran through the park next to the Heyworth Sheriff's Department. Their cries of laughter sent a pang of longing in her heart. She'd visited with Lily this morning, but they hadn't been able to stay for very long. She missed her little girl fiercely.

Cathy, the daytime receptionist, greeted them when they walked inside. Her earrings swayed as she rose from her chair to give Emma a hug. "I'm so sorry about what happened, honey."

"Thank you, Cathy."

"The prayer circle is hard at work and we've already taken up a collection of items at the diner. Clothes, household supplies, toys for Lily. It's not much yet, but it's something to get you started." She stroked Sadie on the head. "I think there's even a doggie bed."

New tears pricked Emma's eyes. She blinked them back. "Thank you so much."

"It's nothing, honey. We take care of our own." The older woman patted Reed on the arm. "I'm so glad you're all okay. Deputy Irving has already called in. I told him to focus on recuperating and we'll call if we need something."

"You did exactly right," Reed said. "Is Cooper here?"

"In the conference room, waiting for y'all. Have you had lunch yet? Should I order something?"

"No, thank you. We were at my aunt's earlier, and she fed us until we nearly exploded."

They all laughed. Emma gave Cathy one more hug and said another thank-you before following Reed to the conference room.

The Texas Ranger looked up when they entered. Cooper was sporting a three-day-old beard and his complexion was pale. At his elbow rested several discarded to-go cups from a local coffee shop. He'd been working the case nonstop, and Emma was certain that, like them, he was running on very little sleep.

Will sat in one of the chairs, typing on a laptop. He barely looked up to greet them. His fingers flew over the keyboard. Sadie walked around him and settled down for a nap in the corner of the room.

"What's going on?" Reed asked.

"We've had a breakthrough in the case," Cooper said. "Will's working on getting us a search warrant."

Emma gripped the back of a chair. "Have you found Mike?"

"Not yet, but we did find where he was staying, thanks to you." Cooper opened a file folder and pulled out several photographs, sliding them across the table. "Since you followed Mike and were able to give a description of the motorcycle as well as the license plate, we put out a BOLO on it. A police officer from nearby Harrisburg spotted the bike sitting at a motel off the highway."

Reed flipped through the photographs before handing them to Emma. The motel was run-down, with chipped paint and slanted numbers on the doors. Mike's motorcycle sat in the parking spot for room 103.

"Mike wasn't in the hotel room, and as often happens in these kinds of places, the front desk clerk didn't know anything about anyone."

"What about security cameras?" Emma asked.

Cooper snorted. "In our dreams. We did obtain a search warrant for the room, however, and found two things of interest."

"What?"

He pushed another photograph across the table. "Two glasses partially filled with beer were on the table. One had Mike's fingerprints. The other had Joshua Lowe's."

Emma sucked in a breath. "So they *do* know each other."

Cooper nodded. "We located a neighbor who was living near the Lowes when Joshua was a kid. She told us Mike and his brother, Charlie, were regular visitors. Joshua's dad and Mike were especially close."

"What else did you find?" Reed asked. "You said there were two things of interest."

Cooper's mouth drew down. Will stopped typing on the laptop. The stillness in the room was unnerving. Emma shifted closer to Reed.

"We found a ton of cash, along with a pile of jewelry," Cooper said, flipping to a new photograph. "Among the items were a set of etched gold hoops."

Emma glanced down at the earrings before focusing on Reed. Recognition flashed across his features. "Are these what I think they are?"

"What?" Emma asked. A sinking feeling settled in the pit of her stomach. "What are they?"

Will cleared his throat. "We have one photograph of Bonnie taken on the day she disappeared by an ATM camera. She was wearing a set of earrings exactly like those."

Cooper ran a hand over his beard. "I had them compared by my analysts at the state lab. The earrings we found and the ones in the photograph from the ATM are consistent."

"So…" Emma picked up the photograph. "These are Bonnie's earrings?"

"Yes. We're getting a search warrant for Joshua's property."

"I want to search it first with Sadie."

"Emma's right," Reed said, before turning to her. "Maybe your theory about my sister being alive was right. We were just looking for her on the wrong property."

She nodded. "That's how her bracelet ended up in my shed. She escaped from Joshua's and made it as far as Uncle Jeb's shed before she was caught again."

Cooper held up a hand. "Guys—"

"You don't have to say it, Cooper." Reed rocked back on his heels. "I know it's a long shot, but it won't harm anything to try. I need to do this."

The Texas Ranger glanced at her. Emma straightened to her full height.

"Sadie and I are ready. Get the search warrant and we'll look for Bonnie."

The wait for the search warrant didn't take long but for Reed, it might as well have been an eternity. He didn't want to get his hopes up. The possibility of Bonnie being alive was slim, but a part of him wouldn't let go of the idea. Only when he had definitive proof would he accept she wasn't coming home again.

Emma sat in the passenger seat, staring out the window.

"You don't have to do this," Reed said as they pulled off the highway and onto the country road leading to Joshua's property. "We can get another team to search."

"No. I wouldn't have agreed if Sadie and I couldn't do it. We want to help, if we can."

Joshua's ranch came into view. The driveway was filled with law enforcement vehicles and several deputies and troopers lingered outside. Reed and Emma had stayed behind, allowing the initial search of the house to take place before they arrived on the premises. It was safer for Emma and Sadie that way.

The carport next to the house was empty. The rain had washed everything clean, and heavy thunderclouds loomed in the distance. The reprieve from the storm was a short one. Cooper stood on the front porch.

"Wait here for a second, Emma," Reed said. "I want to make sure everything is clear with Cooper before we start the search."

She eyed the sky. "Sadie and I can work in the rain, but I'd rather not be out with lightning."

"Understood. I'll be quick."

He left the engine running, so she and Sadie would have cool air. Cooper saw him coming and met him halfway.

"Looks like Joshua isn't home," he said in lieu of a greeting. "According to a ranch hand who works for him here and there, Joshua has had a trip planned for months to attend the cattle auction in Dallas."

"Convenient."

"The timing is suspicious. We still haven't located Mike, so we need to take precautions. There's a possibility he's on the property. Everyone's been instructed to assume Mike is armed and dangerous."

"Emma's wearing protection." Reed glanced back at his vehicle. "I'd try to talk her out of searching again, but I already know she won't listen."

Austin came out of Joshua's house. His expression was stern, but Reed saw the worry hidden in the depths of his cousin's eyes. "Y'all should come inside. There's something you need to see."

The two men joined him inside the house. The living room was rustic, with mismatched furniture and wood paneling on the walls, but it was tidy. The kitchen had crooked wood cabinets and a scratched linoleum floor. The ancient fridge hummed. A mug sat in the sink. Several crime scene technicians were dusting for fingerprints.

Austin led them down a long hallway and they stepped into what Reed surmised was the master bedroom. His eyes widened. Unlike the rest of the house, this room was a wreck. The comforter was piled in a heap on the floor. A lamp, probably from the bedside table, was shattered into pieces. Blood covered some of the shards.

"It appears there was some kind of struggle," Austin said. With a gloved hand, he pointed to the nightstand's half-open drawer. "There's a handgun inside."

Cooper rocked back on his heels. "If Joshua was sleeping in bed, and an intruder startled him, he would go for the gun."

"But the attacker beat him to it, smashing the lamp over his head, possibly knocking him out," Reed finished. "But for what purpose? It doesn't make any sense."

Reed rested his hands on his belt. He wasn't wearing gloves and didn't want to touch anything. Through an opposite doorway, the bathroom was visible. He stepped inside, eyeing the sink and bathtub. "When did Joshua supposedly leave for Dallas?"

"This morning," Cooper replied.

"The sink and bathtub are dry." He eyed the towel hanging on the back of the door. "So is the towel. It doesn't look like he used them."

"But there are empty hangers in the closet. It appears a suitcase is missing. And his car is gone."

Reed stepped back into the bedroom. A photograph overturned from the nightstand lay on the floor. Bonnie stood in a field of bluebonnets. One hand held a wide brimmed hat and the other was outstretched. She was caught mid-laugh, her eyes crinkled with happiness. The echo of Joshua's words swirled in Reed's mind. *I loved her.*

"Maybe Mike attacked him," Cooper suggested.

"And what? Dragged Joshua out to his own vehicle, taking his suitcase for good measure? That makes no sense."

"Criminals do weird stuff."

Reed couldn't argue with that. Sometimes people didn't always react logically.

Austin frowned. "There could be another explanation. I've got an empty bottle of whiskey on this side of the bed. Maybe Joshua got drunk and knocked over the lamp, cutting himself in the process. He got up this morning and ran out of the house to get to the auction without cleaning up."

Reed arched his brows. "That seems more reasonable. Is there a BOLO out for Joshua?"

Cooper nodded. "Yep, and I've got state troopers heading to the cattle auction to ask around for him."

Thunder rolled. Reed glanced at the window. "The storm is coming in. If Emma and Sadie are going to search the property, we need to do it now."

"I'll come with you," Austin said.

"Take a deputy with you," Cooper added. "And be careful. Mike is still out there somewhere."

Emma's fingers shook slightly as she strapped on Sadie's vest. The wind was picking up, adding to her anxiety. Every second counted. If Bonnie was somewhere on the property, Emma wanted to find her now.

"Are you okay?"

Reed's question was low enough only Emma could hear.

Concern darkened the blue of his eyes, and his mouth was set in a grim line. He had to be scared about what they would find on the property, as much as she was, yet he took the time to comfort her.

God, why did you bring him back into my life and then make things so hard? The kiss in Reed's kitchen had been wonderful. It also scared her. She didn't want to end up brokenhearted.

She squared her shoulders. "I'm fine. Let's get started."

She took Sadie to the outer edge of the woods, far away from any deputies searching the house, and gave the command. Her dog headed into the woods.

Emma followed, keeping Sadie in sight. Austin and Reed flanked her, and another deputy she didn't recognize took the rear. The tall pine trees blocked out most of the late afternoon sunlight. Goose bumps broke out across her arms. They were heading toward the back road, the one separating Emma's property from Joshua's.

Sadie stopped and sniffed something. Hidden within the branches and bushes was a huge, lurking object.

"What is that?" Emma frowned. "Is that a car?"

"Yes," Austin answered, his foot crushing a branch. "And by the looks of it, it's been here a while."

It was covered in pine needles and dust. Dead branches obscured the windows and the tires were buried in the bushes. Reed bypassed them both, his long strides covering the distance easily. He bent down and separated some branches to reveal the license plate. "It's my sister's vehicle."

Reed and Austin shared a look. Emma's stomach ached. They pulled on gloves and started peering into the windows. Reed tried a door handle. It creaked open. The car had been left unlocked.

Sadie started barking. With lead feet, Emma circled around to her dog. Her heart stopped and then thundered.

Sadie was signaling at the rear of the vehicle. Emma gave the release command. Her dog immediately backed off. She whined, her ears down.

Oh, no. No.

Emma pulled a treat from the bag at her waist out of habit and tried to give it to Sadie. The dog wouldn't take it. Instead, she whined again. She backed up farther from the car as if wanting as much distance between her and the vehicle as possible. Emma couldn't blame her. She ran her hands over Sadie's soft fur. A prayer left her lips, as automatic as the comfort she gave her dog.

Feet crunched the ground behind her. "There's something in the trunk, isn't there?"

Reed's voice was hollow. Emma bit her lip and turned. Their eyes met. She would spare him this if she could but there was nothing she could do. "Sadie's trained to find live people, but there have been times she's located a recently deceased person."

Had Bonnie been alive until last night? It was possible. Bile rose in Emma's throat.

Reed's spine went rigid. He gestured to the deputy waiting at the driver's side door. "Find the latch to open it."

Austin placed a gloved hand on the trunk. "Reed, maybe you shouldn't be here—"

"Open it, Austin."

The order was sharp and caustic. Reed was holding it together but just barely. Emma reached out. She grasped Reed's hand. His posture didn't change but he interlocked their fingers, drawing her closer until she was at his side. She could feel the tension in his muscles. The pulse at his neck was racing.

Austin sighed and nodded to the deputy. He fumbled before finding the release. The latch snicked and the trunk lid swung open.

Emma gasped.

Mike Young's body was stuffed inside, a bullet wound on his forehead.

SIXTEEN

The next morning, Reed guzzled his third cup of coffee as he paced Aunt Bessie's backyard. Last night's thunderstorms had given way to a beautiful spring day. Bees flitted in a nearby flowerbed. He shifted the cell phone against his ear. "What do we know so far?"

"Well, Mike was killed sometime in the early morning hours yesterday," Cooper said. His voice sounded weary. "Initial ballistics tests conclude the gun in Joshua's nightstand doesn't match the weapon used to kill Mike."

"Maybe Joshua took it with him."

"Possible, but we've got another problem. Joshua never made it to Dallas, and so far, both he and his truck are missing."

Reed's gaze shot to the enclosed porch. Emma was rocking on the swing with Lily in her lap. Vivian leaned on the railing. The two women were having what appeared to be a deep conversation.

"What about the blood on the lamp?" he asked.

"Same blood type as Joshua's, although DNA is going to take a bit longer." Cooper sighed. "I gotta tell you, Reed, something about this isn't sitting right with me. The whiskey bottle we recovered from Joshua's room didn't have any fingerprints on it. It'd been wiped clean. I think it was placed in his room to make us believe the mess was the result of a drinking binge."

Reed's steps faltered. The niggle of doubt he'd been feeling since yesterday in Joshua's house grew. "You think someone's trying to frame him?"

"I think it's something we should consider. Emma and Sadie went over all of Joshua's property yesterday and didn't find a trace of Bonnie other than the car. If that's what Joshua was hiding, why stick Mike in the trunk? It seems like a guaranteed way for us to locate the vehicle."

"He didn't know we'd get a search warrant. Besides, his fingerprints were on the glass in Mike's room."

"About that. We initially thought those glasses were from the hotel. They weren't. We recovered a matching set from Joshua's kitchen cabinet. Normally, that would indicate Joshua took them to Mike's room, but...the move is sloppy. Everything about this perpetrator has proven he's smart. It doesn't fit."

"Let me get this straight. You think someone broke into Joshua's house, attacked him, loaded him into his own truck and...then what? Took some glasses from his kitchen to place in Mike's hotel room?"

"Yes. If we assume for just a moment that Joshua isn't involved, then there's only one person who knew where Bonnie's car was. The person who took her."

Reed set his mug on the concrete sidewalk and rubbed his head. "Cooper, Bonnie's vehicle was parked on Joshua's land."

"We can't assume he knew it was there. That part of the property was overgrown. Without Emma and Sadie, it would've been difficult to find it." Cooper paused for a long beat. "Reed, Judge Norton was at the sheriff's department looking for you this morning."

"I know. He texted me this morning—" Reed cut off,

his tired brain catching up to Cooper's insinuation. "No way."

"I don't like it any more than you do, but we need to keep an open mind. Joshua bought that property from Judge Norton. By all accounts, Bonnie and the judge were close."

"Which doesn't give him motive."

"No, but…"

"Just spit it out, Cooper."

"Will came to me after we located Bonnie's car. He remembered there was a strange incident between Bonnie and his uncle a month or so before her disappearance."

Reed stiffened. This was the first he was hearing about this. "What kind of incident?"

"An argument between Bonnie and the judge. Will wasn't sure what it was about—neither of them would tell him—but he had the vague impression Bonnie was very upset about it. She fled the office as soon as Will arrived."

"That's extremely vague."

"I know. Will was being careful with his wording, but finding Bonnie's car and bracelet in such close proximity to his uncle's land clearly got him thinking."

"We need to take what Will says with a grain of salt. He's had a problematic past with his uncle. Besides, Joshua's the one who asked to buy that piece of property from Judge Norton. Judge Norton wasn't even looking to sell it."

"You're saying Joshua bought it specifically to hide the car?"

"Yep. Ten to one, the technicians will find the car died and wasn't able to be moved without a tow truck. Bonnie's vehicle was a hunk of junk." Reed let out a breath. "There are some other loose threads. What about Bonnie's earrings in Mike's room? And the fact that Joshua couldn't provide an alibi for the time around my sister's disappearance?"

"Trust me, I'm not wiping Joshua off the suspect list. Not by a long shot. I'm just telling you there are inconsistencies in the evidence. He might not be our man."

Reed heard the frustrated note in Cooper's voice. He shared it. "Any news on Owen?"

"No. I've had troopers investigate all of his favorite drinking places. We've talked to his friends and his ex-girlfriends. No one has heard a word from him since he ran away from the hospital."

Another piece of the puzzle that didn't fit. Was Owen behind all of this? Or was Joshua? Or were they overlooking a vital suspect, like Judge Norton?

On the porch, Emma and Vivian's discussion was taking a turn for the worse. Reed was too far away to make out the words, but the stiffness in Emma's shoulders was enough to worry him.

"I'll go talk to Margaret Carpenter again," Reed said. "She was Bonnie's best friend. If there was a problem between Bonnie and Judge Norton, maybe she knows something about it."

"Keep me updated."

"Will do." Reed hung up. He strolled across the yard. Vivian slipped into the house just as he climbed the porch steps.

Emma glanced up as the screen door closed behind him. Lily was sitting in her lap.

"Hey," Reed said, gesturing to the space next to them. "This seat taken?"

"We were saving it for you. What did Cooper say?"

He repeated their conversation. About halfway through, Lily worked her way onto Reed's lap. He tucked the baby into the corner of his arm and rocked the swing. With

Emma nestled on his other side, it felt right. A little whisper of worry told him not to get used to it. Emma was hesitant to give her heart to a man with a risky job. Not that he could blame her. Especially after she'd already lost one husband.

But what if he wasn't in law enforcement anymore? Could he live a happy life working his family's old ranch? He loved being sheriff, but his career had taken a toll on him. Maybe it was time for a change. A slower pace of life. A less dangerous profession. He wouldn't make any decisions until after Bonnie's disappearance was solved, but it was something to consider.

When he was done telling Emma about his conversation with Cooper, she shook her head. "Wow."

"Wow is right."

"I'd like to go with you to talk to Margaret. I know we stayed here last night, but it's probably better for me to stay away from Lily and Vivian until we know what's going on."

"I agree." He paused. "Everything okay with you and Vivian?"

"No." Emma's gaze slid away from his and she bit her lip. "We were talking about what's going to happen next for us."

"What does that mean?"

"We can't keep going like this, Reed. The case keeps stretching out and now my facility and house are gone. I have to start thinking about my family and creating a permanent place for Lily."

He stopped the swing. Lily dropped her toy on the floor. "You're leaving Heyworth?"

"I don't want to, but I may not have any other choice."

"Where will you go?"

The baby started to cry, and Emma handed Lily her

favorite toy. The stuffed lamb was looking worn around the edges. "Vivian's house hasn't sold, so I think we'll go back to Boston."

Boston. It was thousands of miles away. With his sister's case unsolved, Reed couldn't leave town. The pain in the center of his chest radiated out. It hurt so bad, Reed actually looked down at his uniform to make sure he wasn't bleeding. "When?"

"Soon. I want to give it a bit more time, in the hope that the threat can be eliminated and we can stay. I love Heyworth, and as it turns out, Vivian doesn't want to leave either. She and your aunt have discovered a mutual love of cooking. They're talking about opening a restaurant together."

Her voice vibrated with pain. The interaction he'd witnessed between the two women suddenly made sense. "You've done more than your fair share," he said. "I know this hasn't been easy on any of you and the decision is a tough one. I know this isn't what you wanted."

"No, not at all—" Her voice choked off. Emma's gaze dropped to Lily in his arms. The baby hugged her lamb and babbled.

"This was supposed to be your home," he said.

A safe place to raise her daughter and build a life. Now it was a nightmare filled with dead bodies and threats.

"Yes," she whispered. "I thought God had brought me here to settle down and make my life. Now, I'm not sure. Maybe…maybe I was brought here to aid Bonnie's case. I pray finding the car will provide the necessary evidence to locate her."

"Emma…" A lump in his throat choked him. He wanted to ask her to stay. The words burned his tongue, but he swallowed them back. Lily's safety and happiness had to be first. "I hope we can stay in contact and remain friends."

Tears shimmered in her eyes. "Always."

Reed pulled Emma closer, until she was nestled up next to him, and pushed the swing. Her tears wet his shirt. There were no words to make it better. He knew that, but he also knew he had to hold on to this moment. This breath of time when his arms were full with a family he hadn't known until recently he wanted.

Reed didn't know when it happened, but it was as undeniable as the sun. He'd fallen in love. When Emma and Lily left town, they would be taking his heart with them.

Heyworth Veterinarian Clinic smelled like a mixture of wet dog and antiseptic. Sadie's tail went down as they crossed the threshold. The poor dog hated coming here. No amount of treats or reassurance seemed to ease her visits.

"Don't worry," Emma whispered. "No shots today."

Sadie gave her a baleful look. Reed chuckled. "I don't think she believes you."

"I know."

The office was empty. The receptionist's computer flashed with a screen saver. Margaret came around the corner, looking at her phone. Her hair was pulled back into a high ponytail and it bobbed as she drew up short. A hand fluttered to her throat. "Emma. Reed. You startled me."

"We're sorry," Reed said. "The bell rang over the door, and your receptionist is gone."

"All of my staff is at lunch. You didn't have an appointment, did you?" Margaret bent down to stroke Sadie. "Emma, I heard about what happened to your uncle's house. I'm so sorry. It's fortunate Reed was there to help."

"Thank you, Margaret."

Emma refused to allow herself to glance at Reed. If she

did, she feared she might burst into tears. The entire car ride over had been painfully silent. She couldn't blame him for putting up a wall, but it stung all the same.

The memory of their conversation on Aunt Bessie's porch scraped at the raw edges of her heart. The loss of her uncle's home and Helping Paws was devastating. Salt on the wound was saying goodbye to Reed. But Emma didn't see any way around it. She had a daughter to think about, and Reed would never leave Heyworth. Not while his sister's case was still open.

Maybe it was better this way. Better to say goodbye before things got any more serious between them.

"Margaret, we need to ask you a few questions about Bonnie." Reed's tone was blunt. "We located her car."

The veterinarian shot up from her crouch. "Where?"

"Near the back road bordering Joshua's land with Emma's. Can you think of any reason Bonnie would be out that way?"

Her brows drew down. "No. I mean, she used to fish at the lake sometimes. Jeb let her borrow poles from his shed. But I can't imagine she was there late at night."

Emma's hand tightened on Sadie's leash. "You mentioned the last time we talked that you hadn't been aware of Bonnie's relationship with Joshua. Do you know why she kept it secret from you?"

"She knew I wouldn't approve." Margaret's nose wrinkled. "Joshua had a criminal history and was known as something of a bad boy. Bonnie was a sweet girl. She had a soft spot for those with sad stories."

"You think he took advantage of her kindness?"

"I don't know. People often did."

Reed's expression never shifted, but Emma sensed his interest. "Like who?"

Margaret licked her lips. "I wasn't thinking of someone

in particular. Just…people. Bonnie interacted with a lot of the townsfolk because of her work at the courthouse. She was a regular at the sheriff's department. People were always asking her to do favors and stuff like that. She never learned how to say no."

"What was Bonnie's relationship like with Judge Norton?" he asked.

Something flickered in Margaret's expression before she smoothed it out. "I assume it was fine. We didn't talk about it much."

Emma had the distinct sense she was lying. "If you know something, Margaret, you need to say so. We aren't gossiping. We're trying to get to the truth and help Bonnie."

"Of course you are. I'm sorry. This is a small town and things have a way of getting around." Margaret fiddled with her scrub top. "Bonnie had some issues with Judge Norton. She felt he was interested in her…romantically."

Reed stiffened. Emma shifted in front of him. Margaret would have an easier time telling a woman. "Did she ever report it? Judge Norton was her boss."

"No. It was a tough situation. I mean, she'd been dating Will for a long time and she didn't want to hurt him. And the judge was discreet about it. He would massage her shoulders or stroke her hair. It was weird and made Bonnie uncomfortable, but it didn't quite rise to the level of sexual harassment."

Could that have been what the argument between Bonnie and Judge Norton been about? It was possible.

"Did Will know?" Emma asked.

"Bonnie certainty wouldn't have told him. Will is the jealous type and his relationship with his uncle is rocky. Like I said, it made her uncomfortable, but Judge Norton was careful not to cross the line."

"Do you think it's something she would've told Joshua?"

Margaret shrugged. "Honestly, I don't know. Maybe."

They talked for a few more minutes, but Margaret didn't have any other information. They said their goodbyes. Emma waited until they were in Reed's SUV before placing a hand on his arm. "Are you okay?"

He pounded the steering wheel. "There was so much about Bonnie's life I didn't know."

"She was protecting you."

"That wasn't her job." His jaw tightened. "It was mine. I'm her big brother."

"It doesn't work that way, Reed. We always protect those we love. You and I both know, if Bonnie had told you about Judge Norton, you would've confronted him. It's who you are."

He closed his eyes and leaned his head back. "Judge Norton. If what Margaret says is true, Emma, he has motive. If he was interested romantically in Bonnie…"

"Then there's a chance he wanted to prevent her from marrying Joshua. Permanently."

SEVENTEEN

The lamp in the corner of the living room cast a soft glow over the room. Emma lay on the couch, covered in a throw, her dark hair spread across a pillow. She'd fallen asleep reading a book. Sadie lay on the carpet next to her.

Reed shifted the laptop on the rickety tray table. The recliner wasn't the best place to work, but he didn't consider moving. Silly perhaps, and more than a little sentimental, but he wanted to be near Emma.

His phone beeped with an alert from his security system, indicating activity near the house. Reed pulled up the camera and saw Austin getting out of his truck. His hand tightened on the phone. Austin had been in charge of coordinating the search of Joshua's property. Had the cadaver dogs found anything?

Reed disarmed the house alarm and met Austin at the door. "Shhh, Emma fell asleep on the couch."

Austin removed his cowboy hat and hung it on a hook next to the door. In his other hand was a takeout bag from a fast-food restaurant. The scent of fries tickled Reed's nose. He gave his cousin a questioning look.

Austin shook his head. "They didn't find anything," he whispered.

Reed let out a breath. The two men went into the kitchen.

Austin opened the fridge and pulled out a soda. Sadie wandered in and beelined for the back door.

"You need to go out, girl?" Reed asked. He opened the screen door for her, and she dashed out. Reed's phone beeped with an alert. He ignored it. The cameras were picking up Sadie's jaunt through the yard.

"What's the latest, Austin?"

"There isn't much that's new. The cadaver team isn't finished. They've done about half the property. The rest will be done tomorrow." Austin unwrapped a burger and bit into it. "We did find several more handguns in the house. They were in the basement. Cooper has sent them to the lab to be tested."

Which meant Joshua could've shot Mike, they just didn't have the proof yet. "How soon before we get the results?"

He shrugged. "Tomorrow sometime. He's put a rush on it."

"Did Cooper tell you about his theory? That Judge Norton might be involved?"

"Yes. He also informed me about what Margaret told you."

"I've done some additional digging. Hold on." Reed retrieved a file folder from his home office. "All of them—Vernon, Mike and Charlie—appeared in Judge Norton's courtroom."

"So have most of the criminals in the county." Austin dunked several fries into some ketchup.

"Yes, but these men never were sentenced harshly. They've committed crime after crime, but only received a slap on the wrist each time."

It didn't sit right with him. It was almost as if the men were being protected. Not all of the cases appeared before

Judge Norton, but it would've have been difficult for him to put in a word with the other judges.

"Listen, Reed, we need to pursue every avenue, but I think you and Cooper are barking up the wrong tree with this one. Judge Norton doesn't have so much as a speeding ticket. I can't see him kidnapping Bonnie or killing her."

"You know as well as I do, sometimes evil resides in a place you would least expect."

Austin wiped his hands on a napkin and flipped through some of the records on the table. "Look at this. Deputy Hendricks arrested both Mike and Charlie at different points. Will was the prosecutor on several of these cases. If you're looking for connections, they're all over the place. We aren't that big of a department or a county. You'll need a lot more than this to accuse a sitting judge."

"We aren't looking to accuse him of anything," Reed corrected. "And no one knows we're looking into Judge Norton except for a small group of people. For obvious reasons."

Emma came into the kitchen, squinting at the light. "What's going on?"

"We're just discussing the case."

The fog in her expression lifted when her gaze fell on Austin. She stiffened. "Did—"

"No," he said quickly. "The cadaver dogs didn't find Bonnie."

"Well, that's a relief." She rubbed her face. "Is Sadie in here with you guys? I woke up on the couch and she wasn't in the living room."

"I let her out," Reed said. He got up and opened the back door, but the dog wasn't in the yard. His phone beeped with a new notification. An unfamiliar truck was making its way up his driveway. "Someone's coming."

Austin stood and joined him at the front door. Sadie

raced up the steps and Emma let her inside. The flood-lights clicked on. Wayne Johnson dropped out of the cab. The ranch hand was wearing a dusty set of overalls and a bandanna around his neck. His shotgun was attached to a rack on his truck.

"Sorry to disturb you so late, Sheriff."

"That's all right. What's going on?"

Wayne settled his hands on his hips. "Well, now, after our discussion down by the lake the other day, I got to thinking you needed to talk to Owen. I remembered Jeb mentioned he had an aunt in Livingston. I gots to thinkin' maybe Owen was hiding out there."

The screen door creaked as Emma joined them on the porch. "I thought Mabel was dead."

"No, ma'am. She's over ninety, but she's still alive and well. Anyway, I ventured out there and talked with her."

Reed drew up to his full height. "Wayne, you shouldn't have done that."

He lifted a hand. Dirt was embedded in the skin of his fingers, staining them darker than his palm. "Don't be warmin' up for a lecture, Sheriff. I did what I thought was best. Owen is as jittery as an untrained coonhound. The last thing he needed was people showing up with guns blazing."

Reed wanted to tell the ranch hand they wouldn't have gone in guns blazing, but it would've fallen on deaf ears. Some of the citizens of Heyworth were used to taking matters into their own hands. Wayne was one of them. "Did you find Owen?"

"I did. He's in the truck."

Reed's hand immediately went to his weapon, although he left it in the holster. Wayne waved at the vehicle.

The rear door on the extended cab opened. Owen appeared. His hands were held up in a classic sign of surrender.

"It took a bit of talkin' but I convinced him you were good folks who would hear him out," Wayne said. "Don't make a liar out of me. And, Sheriff, trust me. You want to hear what he has to say."

Reed nodded. He went down the porch steps. Owen watched him approach with a wary expression, but his eyes were clear and focused. He appeared sober, which was a good start. Still, the man was criminal and had run away from the law. There was only so much leeway Reed would give him.

"Owen, I need to check you for weapons but then we'll all go inside and talk."

Owen nodded. Within a few minutes, they were settled around the kitchen table. The coffeepot gurgled. Emma bustled around pulling down mugs and plating some cookies.

"Where have you been?" Reed asked.

"A rehab facility in Houston." Owen shifted in the chair. "I was wrong to escape from the hospital, especially since I was under arrest, but Vernon and Mike were looking for me. They wanted to kill me."

Emma froze, before handing a mug of coffee to her cousin. "Why would they want you dead?"

"I'm Joshua's alibi for the night Bonnie disappeared."

Owen's words had the effect of a bomb going off. Everyone was still and quiet. Reed leaned in. "If that's so, why is this the first I'm hearing about it?"

"Because I made Joshua promise to keep it a secret. The night of Bonnie's disappearance, I was with Mike. We broke into a house on Franklin Street. The owners were supposed to be gone, but I guess the husband stayed behind for some reason. We got caught. Mike escaped, but the husband beat me pretty badly before I was able to get out of the house."

Reed glanced at Austin. His cousin nodded. "There was a robbery that night. The owner couldn't identify the two men, but he did mention beating one of them pretty good."

"I couldn't go to the hospital, for obvious reasons," Owen said. "Mike had taken the truck and disappeared. I was desperate and called the only person I could think of to help me. Joshua used to rob houses with us but he stopped a long time ago. Still, I figured he would give me a ride."

"And did he?"

Owen nodded. His shaggy hair fell into his eyes. "Although Joshua was upset about it. He warned me it was the last time he would help me. He advised me to straighten out my life. Anyway, I'm the reason Joshua was late to meet Bonnie at the park. We went there together but she was already gone. Joshua tried calling her a few times, but she didn't answer. He was worried she'd think he'd gotten cold feet."

Reed made a point to keep his expression impassive, but if Owen was telling the truth, then Joshua couldn't have hurt Bonnie. And if Joshua wasn't behind his sister's disappearance, then someone else was.

Maybe Judge Norton's involvement wasn't such a stretch, after all.

Sadie nudged Emma's hand with her head, and she stroked her dog's soft fur. She took a sip of her coffee, but it swirled in her stomach like battery acid. Owen's delay in providing an alibi for Joshua may have caused serious harm. Joshua was missing, after all. She could only hope he was hiding out and not hurt or dead.

"What time did Joshua drop you off?" Reed asked.

"Late. I'm not sure. He was going to drive over to Bonnie's apartment to see if she was there. He was frantic. I was too messed up at the time, but in the morning, I felt really bad. Especially when I heard about her disappearance."

"Why didn't you come forward when she went missing?"

"Because I didn't want to be arrested for the robbery. Joshua and I had several arguments about it—the most recent one happened on the same day I confronted Emma on the porch."

Emma's gaze flickered to Wayne. It was the fight the ranch hand had observed and told them about.

"Joshua wanted me to come forward and explain he had an alibi," Owen continued. "He knew you wouldn't give up on finding Bonnie, Reed. But Joshua was worried time and energy was being wasted looking into him. I refused. I knew Joshua wouldn't say anything either because he'd given his word to me."

Emma pushed away her coffee. "Why come forward now?"

"Because Joshua was right. It's time I straighten out my life. Getting sober is the first step, but I also need to take responsibility for my actions."

Reed drummed his fingers on the table. "I heard you and Bonnie had an altercation a few months before her disappearance?"

Owen blanched. "We did. I was drunk and it shouldn't have happened. Drinking has gotten me into a lot of trouble." He took a deep breath. "I owe you a huge apology, Emma. I treated you badly. I was angry and hurt, but that's no excuse."

His voice rang with shame and regret. She closed her eyes. Holding on to her anger wouldn't get them anywhere. Owen's addiction had caused him to make choices she knew in her heart weren't true to who he was as a person. "Apology accepted. All I wanted—all Uncle Jeb wanted—was for you to be healthy."

"I know that now."

Wayne took a cookie from the plate in the center of the table. "Tell the sheriff what you told me, Owen. He needs to know the rest."

"There's more?" Reed asked.

Owen scratched his chin. "Being arrested for the robbery wasn't the only reason why I didn't want to come forward. Dean Shadwick is the other. He's a dirty cop."

Emma's posture went rigid. Dean was the deputy she'd filed a complaint with after someone tried to poison Sadie.

"How do you know this?" Reed demanded.

"Because he's the one who introduced me to Mike Young. Dean's been working with the Young brothers for a long time. Lately, they've been cooking meth and selling it in the next county."

Emma let out a breath. "That's why Dean was so protective of you when I initially reported the stalking on my property. You knew his secrets."

"Not all of them, but enough to count."

"Dean always was a sneaky one," Wayne said. "His daddy was a good man, but my wife used to teach in the high school and she never trusted Dean further than she could throw him. Many townsfolk didn't like it when the former sheriff hired him to be a deputy."

Austin was silent, but from the hard line of his mouth, Emma was sure he had a few choice words to share with them in private. He probably knew more since he'd worked with Dean for a longer period of time than Reed had.

"Deputy Shadwick did a lot of work on Bonnie's case." She frowned. "His name appeared on most of the reports."

"That's because he headed up the investigation," Austin said. "The former sheriff insisted on it. At the time, I thought it was odd. Dean had little to no experience investigating such a serious crime."

Owen cleared his throat. "There's something else. Dean bragged about working with someone higher up. Someone who would always protect them."

Reed's brows shot up. "Who?"

"I don't know. He never would say, but he made it clear they wouldn't be punished seriously if they ever got caught. It was how he convinced me to get in on some of the crimes."

Reed's phone trilled. He pulled it from his hip and answered the call. Aunt Bessie's voice spilled from the speaker. Emma couldn't make out the words, but they were rushed. Her spine stiffened. Nothing good could come from a call at nearly midnight.

She leaned closer to listen in. Reed took the hint and put the call on speaker. "Aunt Bessie, slow down and tell me exactly what's going on."

"I don't know what's going on." She sucked in a big breath. "I went to bed early and woke up to someone in my room. He attacked me."

Austin grabbed his phone. Within seconds he was snapping out orders in the corner of the kitchen.

"He must've hit me over the head because I don't remember a whole lot," Aunt Bessie continued. "I woke up locked in my closet. I managed to get out, but the trooper outside… He's unconscious and bleeding, Reed."

Emma's body went cold. "Bessie, where are Lily and Vivian?"

Reed placed a hand on Emma's arm, the warmth of his palm a stark contrast to the chills racing through her body.

The sound of running came over the line. Doors opened and closed as Aunt Bessie yelled their names. The panic in the woman's voice added to Emma's. She clamped her lips together to prevent the scream bubbling inside her from tearing loose.

Aunt Bessie started sobbing. "Reed, they aren't here. Lily and Vivian are gone. They've been kidnapped."

EIGHTEEN

Reed raced down the country road, lights flashing and siren blaring. After the phone call from his aunt, they'd received one from Deputy Kyle Hendricks. Aunt Bessie's car—stolen from her house—was spotted on a rarely used back road. It was four in the morning, but still pitch-black outside.

"Hold on," he said to Emma. She gripped the handle above the door as he took a right turn. His tires bounced over a pothole. Sadie, strapped in the back seat, swayed. Behind them, Austin followed in his patrol car.

"This is Old Man Franklin's land," Emma said. Her face was pale and her lips drawn tight. "Isn't that the property Joshua mentioned he bought when I wouldn't sell?"

"Yes."

Reed's hands tightened on the steering wheel until his knuckles were white. Someone had attacked his aunt. Assaulted a trooper. Taken Vivian and Lily. A blinding rage unlike any he'd ever experienced threatened to take hold, but he battled it back. There was no room for emotion. Right now, he needed to focus on getting Emma's family back.

The road curved and the trees parted. A patrol car sat behind Aunt Bessie's sedan. Kyle raised a hand to shield his eyes from the approaching headlights. Reed slammed on the brakes. He flipped off the engine but didn't bother to take the keys out of the vehicle. His boots hit the dirt with a thump.

"There's no one in the car," Kyle said. The deputy struggled to catch up to Reed's long strides. "I already looked."

He didn't care. At this moment, Reed wasn't sure he could trust anyone besides his cousin and Cooper. He quickly walked around his aunt's sedan. The outside appeared untouched. "How did you know the car was here?"

"I got a call from Dean Shadwick."

Emma ran up, catching the last bit of his deputy's answer. She inhaled sharply.

Kyle's brows clashed together. "What's going on?"

Reed had no intention of answering him. "When?" he barked. "When did Dean call you?"

"Right after the BOLO on your aunt's vehicle went out. He mentioned he'd heard about it on his scanner."

"He's suspended."

"He has a police scanner in his personal vehicle."

Reed yanked on a pair of gloves and opened the sedan's driver side door. The overhead light flickered on. Keys were in the ignition.

"I've got what looks like blood," Austin said quietly. Reed's gaze shot to the back seat. A dark stain spread across the leather, dripping down toward the carpet.

Emma cried out. Reed caught her as she rushed toward the vehicle. She wasn't wearing gloves. He couldn't let her accidentally disturb evidence they may need. She gripped his biceps, her fingers clawing into his skin through his shirt.

"Lily's lamb." Tears streamed down her face.

Austin reached in and pulled the familiar stuffed animal

from the floorboard. Reed's own knees weakened but he forced himself to block it out. His gaze swung toward Kyle.

"Did you check the trunk?" he demanded.

Emma slapped a hand over her mouth. Reed kept an arm around her waist, holding her up.

Kyle's face was stark in the headlights. "Yes. It's clear."

Emma shuddered against Reed. He wanted to tell her to wait in his SUV, but there was no way she would listen. Not that he could blame her.

"What did Dean tell you specifically, from start to finish?" Reed asked his deputy.

Kyle straightened. "He called my personal phone and stated that he'd heard the BOLO on the scanner. Dean mentioned he was on his way back from a fishing trip and used this road to cut across town. He spotted the vehicle and said I should check it out because it matched the description."

There was no way Dean was simply coming back from a fishing trip. Reed hadn't been convinced of Owen's claim that Dean was a dirty cop until this moment. Reed had no doubt he'd driven the car here and called his friend to find it. "Did Dean say where he was going?"

"I assumed home." Kyle's gaze flickered to Emma before settling back on Reed. "I thought it was strange he was coming back so late from a fishing trip, but I didn't question it."

No, he wouldn't think to challenge his good friend and fellow deputy. Dean had been counting on that.

A state vehicle slid to a stop and Cooper got out. The Texas Ranger's stride was furious, his hands balled into fists. "What do we have?"

Reed got him up to speed. Cooper stepped over to look at the vehicle himself. Kyle followed. Their flashlights bounced off the chrome bumper of Aunt Bessie's car.

Emma shivered again. Her face was drained of all color and, when Reed touched her skin, she was frigid. He shrugged off his jacket and wrapped it around her before pulling her into his arms. Sirens wailed in the distance.

"Hold on, Em. We've got backup coming and every available unit working on this."

"I don't know if I can keep it together, Reed. My little girl—" Her voice choked off.

"Lily is in God's hands. He's watching over her. I know it's hard, but your faith has pulled you through so much. It will get you through this, too."

She took a deep breath. Then another. Reed rested his head against hers and closed his eyes. He quietly whispered a prayer. It was as much for him as it was for Emma. Lily had stolen his heart and the idea of anything happening to the little girl was enough to cripple him. But what he'd said to Emma came from the depths of his own faith. It was the mantra that got him through the long nights after Bonnie's disappearance. No matter where his sister was, Bonnie was in the Lord's hands and He would see her through.

Emma cupped his cheek with her hand. "Thank you, Reed. I needed the prayer."

"So did I."

A shout from Cooper drew his attention. Releasing Emma, Reed snapped back into professional mode. "What is it?"

"I've got drag marks." Cooper's flashlight drifted across the tall grass a short distance from Aunt Bessie's car. "They disappear into the woods."

Emma raced to Reed's SUV. She unhooked Sadie.

Reed studied the marks. "Those are obvious. The perpetrator wanted us to find them. He practically hung a sign."

"No kidding." Cooper frowned. "It could be a trap, a way to lure Emma and Sadie into the woods."

"It doesn't matter," Emma said. "We still have to go."

Sweat dripped down Emma's back despite the chill in the air. The Kevlar vest was heavy and more than uncomfortable. With every step, it pressed down on her shoulders. The woods were a tangle of limbs and bushes in the faint glow of the moonlight. Sadie's collar jangled.

Reed's flashlight led the way. He'd insisted on walking ahead of her for safety. Arguing would've eaten precious time, and Emma wasn't willing to waste a minute of it. She needed to keep moving. Each step brought her closer to Lily and Vivian. At least, she hoped so.

The sound of running water reached her ears.

"What is that?" she asked.

"There's a natural spring on the property. It feeds into a river," Austin answered. He was behind her, providing cover from any potential attack. "Teenagers often come here to tube down it when Old Man Franklin says it's okay."

Sadie barked.

Reed stopped short. Emma bumped into the back of him. His flashlight beam bounced off the dog's reflective vest.

"I don't see Vivian," Emma said.

Austin pointed. "There."

A tree curved at the water's edge. Some of the branches drifted into the water. Vivian was balanced precariously on the edge of one. She was unconscious, and when Reed's flashlight drew close to her face, Emma's throat clenched. Her sister-in-law had been beaten. Badly. Sadie barked again.

"Where's Lily?" Reed said.

They scanned the immediate area but saw no sign of the little girl. Emma refused to even consider her daughter had been out there on the branch with Vivian but had already fallen in the water. No, she had to focus on one thing at a time. Otherwise she would collapse and wail a mountain of grief.

They scrambled down the bank. Emma took a few precious moments to praise her dog. Reed had pulled his weapon and was keeping watch on their immediate area.

"There's no way to reach her without climbing out on the branch," Austin said. "I don't have rope in my bag. Anyone else?"

Reed shook his head. "We need to call for backup."

They'd purposefully refused to allow troopers and other deputies to traipse through the property since Sadie could search the area faster. Emma sent up a prayer of thanksgiving. It would've taken hours to find Vivian without the dog, and her sister-in-law would've probably died.

"We don't have time to wait for backup." She tore at the straps of her bulletproof vest. "Reed, you hold on to me while I climb out to get her."

"No," Austin said. "I'll go."

"That branch looks ready to break off. It won't support your weight. Or Reed's. I'm the lightest one. I have to go."

Reed's mouth tightened. She felt he wanted to argue with her, but he couldn't deny physics. She dropped the Kevlar vest on the ground. Bark bit into her hand as she shimmed her way into position. Underneath her, the water in the river swirled. It was black as ink. Spring-fed meant it was cold, too.

"Slow and steady," she muttered to herself. "Okay, Reed, hold on to my feet."

His hands grasped her ankles. The grip was firm and

steady. It grounded her. Emma eased out on the branch. It swayed closer to the water.

"Vivian, can you hear me? I'm coming to get you. Don't move."

Her sister-in-law stayed motionless. Only the faint movement of her chest indicated she was breathing and not dead. Emma clung on to that fact. She crept out farther. Her hand strained forward, but Vivian was just out of reach.

The branch creaked. Emma glanced behind her. "Reed, you have to back off. Your weight is too much."

"No. I'm not letting you go."

"There's no other choice. I need a few more inches and then I've got her."

A long pause followed. Reed's hand let go of her left ankle. He flattened himself out, spreading his weight as much as possible. "Try now."

Bark scraped against her stomach. Something tickled the back of her neck. A pine needle or a bug, she couldn't tell. Emma blocked it all out, focusing on reaching Vivian. Her fingertips brushed against her sister-in-law's.

Just a little more.

A resounding crack broke through her concentration. Vivian tumbled away and Reed's cry followed. Her ankle was ripped from his hand.

The world spun. A slap of cold water stole the breath from her lungs. Darkness covered her and, for a heart-stopping moment, she wasn't sure which way was up. Then she hit bottom.

Shoving against the mud, Emma shot herself upward. She surfaced, coughing, and dragged in a breath. The current pulled her downstream. Vivian. Where was Vivian? She twisted in the darkness, searching. Her tennis shoes and clothes dragged her down. She dunked under the cold water.

Lord, please, help me.

She kicked off her tennis shoes and resurfaced. Sucking in a breath, she yelled Reed's name, although it felt like the wind and the current stole it from her. Her fingers brushed against a tangle of something. Seaweed? No, hair. Emma grabbed a handful and yanked. Vivian popped up although her sister-in-law was deathly pale and still unconscious.

"Emma!" Reed yelled from the shoreline.

"I'm here," she cried. Her limbs were going numb, yet she fought to keep Vivian's head above water. Emma couldn't tell if Vivian was breathing. The current thrashed them. Lights to the left indicated Reed and Austin were running along the edge ahead of her.

Rocks. Huge lurking objects in their path. Emma kicked but the river was too difficult to fight. She twisted, using her body to block Vivian from being battered against the stone. Her shoulder whammed against rock. Pain vibrated through her. She gritted her teeth and reached out blindly. Her fingers caught a groove. She held on.

The beam of a flashlight bounced toward her. Emma blinked rapidly to clear the water from her eyes. Reed balanced on a rock. His position was precarious. The surface was wet and smooth as glass.

"Take Vivian," she shouted. Emma struggled to keep her sister-in-law's head above water. Her arm trembled from the cold and exhaustion.

Reed bent down. Water stained his pants leg, turning the fabric dark. With one hand, he grasped Emma's wrist and leaned across to grab hold of Vivian.

"I can't…" His face reddened with the effort. Austin appeared behind him, but the rock wasn't large enough for both men to balance. He couldn't hold on to Emma and pull Vivian from the water. Not at the angle he was at.

"Take her first," she yelled. Vivian wouldn't survive if she was lost in the water. "I can't hold her much longer."

Reed nodded. He released her arm. "Don't you dare let go. Hang on for me, Em."

She was trying, but her fingers were already growing numb. Reed used both hands to yank Vivian from the water. He stood and handed her to Austin. The chief deputy cradled her as if she was more delicate than spun glass.

Emma's hand slipped. A fresh wave of adrenaline shot through her veins. Reed gave a shout. He lunged for her, slipping on the wet stone, and nearly fell into the water. His hand clasped over her wrist.

"I've got you, Em. I've got you."

Reed pulled her from the cold water. He swung an arm under her legs and delicately balanced along the rocks until they hit the shoreline. Emma collapsed on the bank, gasping for breath. Her heart thundered in her ears. She couldn't feel her toes. Austin immediately started CPR on Vivian.

Reed yanked the jacket off Emma's shoulders, replacing it with a blanket. "We need to get you warm, Em."

Her teeth chattered. Sadie licked her face. Someone coughed and vomited. It was the sweetest sound Emma had ever heard. She pushed the dog out of the way. "Vivian?"

Her sister-in-law was tucked against Austin's chest. Her blond hair clung to her face in strings. Somehow it made the bruising on her cheek and the black eye worse. Despite being tossed in the river, blood still stained her pajama top.

Reed pulled another blanket from his backpack and covered Vivian with it. Emma scooted across the distance between them.

"Li-Li-Lily?" Vivian gasped.

"We haven't found her." Emma took Vivian's hand. "What happened?"

"T-t-took her from me. Hurt me. Fight. Don't take the b-b-baby."

Emma's chin trembled. Of course Vivian would've fought fiercely to protect Lily. She'd nearly paid with her life.

"S-s-sorry."

"No. You have nothing to be sorry for. We'll find her, Vivian." Water dripped on their conjoined hands and it took Emma a moment to realize she was crying. "Just like we found you, we'll find Lily."

A phone trilled. Surprise flashed across Reed's face. "That sounds like it's coming from Vivian."

With trembling fingers, Emma lowered the blanket covering her sister-in-law. Vivian was wearing two shirts, a tank top under a pajama button-down. A dark string hung around her neck and disappeared into the button-down. Emma pulled on it. A cell phone came out, secured in a water-proof pouch.

Reed took over. He yanked the phone free of the pouch and answered the call, putting it on speaker so everyone could hear.

"Well, hello, Sheriff." The voice was mangled by a digital voice distorter, making it unrecognizable. "As nice as it is to hear your voice, you aren't the one I'm interested in talking to. Put Emma on the phone."

Reed's gaze shot to her and she grabbed the phone. Her daughter's life was on the line. Whatever the kidnapper wanted, she would give it to him.

"I'm here," Emma said.

"Good. How is your sister-in-law?"

"She's fine, no thanks to you. What do you want?"

"All in good time, Emma. All in good time. First, we need to make something clear. Vivian's bruises, along with her dip in the river, was a message. I'm capable of harming everything that is dear to you."

Goose bumps broke out across Emma's skin. This entire scenario was a setup, designed to terrify her into submission. "You didn't need to bother. I would do anything for my daughter. If you wanted me to follow orders, all you had to do was call."

He chuckled. It was cold and manic. The thought of sweet Lily being with this monster made bile rise in Emma's throat. Reed met her gaze. In the depths of his blue eyes, she saw the strength she needed to hold it together.

"I'm glad we understand each other," the voice said over the phone. "Now, listen closely. Something very important to me was found on your property and I want it returned."

She frowned. "Bonnie's bracelet?"

"That's right. I want it back."

He was crazy. Absolutely nuts. "I don't have it. The police—"

"Took it to the state lab. I know. That's why I need you to get it back for me."

Reed waved a hand, indicating she should stall. Emma swallowed. "That's difficult. I'm not allowed to handle evidence."

"Don't insult my intelligence," he snapped. "Reed can get it for you. And you better pray he does because your daughter's life depends on it."

Anger vibrated in his voice. Emma swallowed hard. "Okay. Okay. I'll get it. Just please don't hurt her."

"Don't make me. Do as I say and everything will be fine. Bring Bonnie's bracelet to the lake on your property in an hour. You will come alone. No bullet-proof vests and no tricks. If I see the sheriff or any of his men, there will be a penalty."

"I'm in the middle of the woods. I'll need more than an hour."

"One hour or else."

A click punctuated his words, followed by the sound of a dial tone.

NINETEEN

A soft pink glow from the rising sun shimmered along the trees. Emma parked her car along the back road separating her property from Joshua's. She glanced at her watch. Ten minutes until her hour grace period was up. She needed to move fast. It would take time to traverse the path through the woods to the lake.

Leaves crunched under Emma's ballerina flats. They were slippery and a poor choice for a hike, but she had little choice. Her tennis shoes were still floating down the river. Vivian had been taken by ambulance to the hospital. Emma wanted to be there with her, but she hadn't had an option about that either.

She gripped the burner phone provided by the killer in her left hand. It was untraceable. She knew. They'd already tried. Cooper was fit to be tied. Reed, too, for that matter. Neither one of them had been comfortable obeying the killer's orders. Emma knew the two men were trying to protect her, but nothing was more important than getting Lily into safe hands. She would not risk her daughter's life by having a SWAT team surrounding the lake.

Her gaze darted around. The hair on the back of her neck rose. A nearby bush rustled. Emma spun in time to see a squirrel dart across the path. She closed her eyes and took a deep breath. Fear threatened to cloud her mind. She wrestled it back. Her jean pocket bulged with Bonnie's bracelet. It'd taken a trooper, even with lights and siren going, forty-five minutes to travel the distance between the state lab and Heyworth.

The trees thinned, revealing the clearing and the lake. Bird flittered above her. Emma hesitated. Once she stepped into the clearing, she'd be exposed. There was little doubt her stalker would be watching. A single shot was all it would take.

You can do this. You have to do this.

Her hand drifted to the zippered pocket of her light jacket and brushed against a familiar lump. Lily's lamb. She took another deep breath to settle her nerves. Saying a quick prayer for her daughter's safety, Emma stepped into the early morning sunshine.

The burner phone rang. She answered it, her voice cracking. "Yes."

"You're late." Same voice distorter, but Emma sensed a desperation in the man's voice that hadn't been there before. It fueled her anxiety. Desperation could cause him to make drastic decisions.

Keep calm. Keep him talking. Stall.

Reed's advice replayed in her mind. Thinking of the handsome sheriff threatened to shred the last of her frayed emotions. Emma wanted him with her. Right next to her, holding her hand. She hadn't realized until now how much comfort she drew from Reed's quiet strength. Emma was tough, she could stand on her own, but she didn't want to anymore.

She forced the thoughts back and cleared her throat. "Sorry for the delay. It took time to get the bracelet."

Could Cooper and his team in the van a mile away hear her through the listening device hidden under her shirt?

She had no idea. Having an earpiece to hear them would've been nice. It was also too risky. They didn't know how close she would get to the killer.

"Where is it?" he demanded.

She tugged Bonnie's bracelet free from her pocket and held it up. The diamond cross winked in the sunlight.

A sigh came over the line. "Good. That's good."

He was definitely watching. She scanned the trees again but saw nothing out of the ordinary. "Why do you want it?"

"What difference does it make to you?"

"My daughter was kidnapped for it. Color me curious."

He chuckled. "I'm sure you are, but that's not part of our deal. Now, I want you to take the bracelet and put it back in the fishing shed."

Her gaze darted to the building across the clearing. Was this some kind of trap? Was the killer in the shed? She couldn't make heads or tails of this. "I want Lily back first."

"No. I told you. I get the bracelet, then you get your daughter. Don't make me angry, Emma."

The coldness in his tone sent a fresh wave of panic through her. She couldn't push him too hard. Getting the truth wasn't worth risking Lily's life.

The spring sunshine swept her shoulders as she crossed the field. Dandelion fluff danced in the air. Somewhere in the lake, a fish jumped. Was Lily nearby? Was her baby hungry? Or hurt? The thoughts raced around inside her head and Emma was powerless to stop them.

She paused outside the shed door. It was cracked open. Although the raccoon had been removed, the scent of death still lingered. Emma's stomach churned. Her hand tightened even more on the burner phone. It was a wonder she didn't snap the thing in two.

"What are you waiting for?" he growled in her ear.

To be ambushed. The words caught in her throat and she swallowed them down. Emma raised a trembling hand. The wood of the shed door under her fingertips was cool to the touch. She shoved. Fishing poles clattered to the ground as the door banged against the opposite wall.

Emma blinked. The shed was empty.

In her ear, the killer chuckled. "Gotcha."

Emma gritted her teeth together. He was somewhere nearby, watching, relishing in her terror. No more. She wouldn't give him the pleasure. She threw the bracelet inside.

"There." She turned in the doorway and jutted up her chin. "It's done. Now give me my daughter."

"Very well."

"How—" She paused. What was that?

Faint crying came from around the corner. Lily! Emma raced behind the building. The sound grew louder, her daughter's cries coming from the trees on the edge of Judge Norton's property.

Emma's shoes slid on the dewy grass as she ran toward the sound. "I'm coming, Lily. I'm coming."

She got closer. Her gaze swept the ground, searching for her baby's small form. Was she okay? Was she crawling among the pine needles?

The cries grew louder. They tore at Emma. "No, baby, don't cry. Mommy's here. Everything's going to be okay—"

She drew up short. On the ground was a recorder. Lily's cries grew frantic, louder, before cutting off completely.

Emma stared in disbelief. "No, no, no."

A branch snapped behind her. Emma whirled but it was too late. Something slammed down on her head. She saw stars and her knees collapsed. A rock on the ground jabbed her in the ribs. Emma inhaled sharply.

She swung out with her fists, but the attacker yanked her by the hair. An arm wrapped around her chest, locking her arms next to her body. The breath was squeezed from her. Her back was slammed up against a man's hard form.

The unmistakable sensation of a gun's barrel pressed against her temple. "Don't move."

She froze. The sound of her own frantic heartbeat roared in her ears. It was so loud, she almost didn't hear the attacker's next words. His breath was hot against her face. "Sheriff! I will shoot her. It's time to come out now."

Quakes overtook Emma. She knew that voice. Recognized the distinctive and cultured Southern drawl immediately, even without seeing his face.

Will Norton.

"He's not here," Emma said. "You told me not to bring anyone."

Please, Lord, keep Reed away from here.

The lake was a huge area. It wasn't possible for one man to cover all of it at once. Plus Emma had disappeared from sight by entering the woods.

Will yanked her free of the trees. "Look what I caught!"

"Let her go, Will." Reed roared from the tree line. "We've got you surrounded."

"Don't play me for a fool. Backup is nowhere close. I've made sure of that. Now come out where I can see you."

"No!" Emma yelled. "Don't."

She didn't need to be told what would happen next. Will had drawn them into a trap, just as Reed had suspected. There was little chance they would both walk out of this alive.

Reed ignored her. He appeared several meters away, his gun drawn. There was no fear in his expression. His mouth was hard, his stance confident. Sunlight played along the chiseled edges of his features and bounced off the sheriff's badge pinned to his chest.

He was a protector. Her protector. Reed couldn't hide in the woods, any more than he could stop breathing. It was who he was.

And she was in love with him.

It hit Emma with the force of a punch to the gut. The depth of her emotions had been lingering below the surface, but she'd refused to acknowledge them. Because she was scared. Because she'd walked through the pain of loss and wasn't sure she could do it again.

But it was there. She was in love with Reed.

And Will was going to kill him.

Things had unraveled within a blink of an eye. One minute Emma was crossing the field toward the shed, the next she was darting into a copse of trees. Reed had lost her in the woods and those precious seconds had given Will the opening he needed to attack.

Reed kept his gun trained on the county prosecutor. He stepped out farther into the clearing. It was risky. There was no way to know if Dean was hiding somewhere nearby with a rifle, just waiting to take him out. But he didn't think it was a strong possibility.

Will wouldn't have done his own dirty work unless he was out of options.

Reed spared one quick glance at Emma. Blood dripped from a wound on her head. She was pale, but her hands were fisted at her sides. That was his Em. Terrified but ready to fight. Will pressed the handgun harder against her temple. Rage raced through Reed's veins. His vision narrowed.

"Drop it, Will."

"Good try, Reed, but that's a no-go. Unless you want

me to shoot Emma right here in front of you, you'll do everything I say. Put your gun down on the ground. Nice and slow."

Reed's hand tightened on his weapon. He couldn't put down his gun. Will would only shoot him and then Emma. "What are you doing, Will?"

"I said put your gun down!"

Reed shifted again. He didn't have a clear shot. Will was using Emma as a human shield. There was no way to take him down without hurting her in the process.

He needed to stall and give his backup time to arrive. Cooper had to be on his way. Emma was wearing a wire.

"I'm serious, Reed." Will said. "I'll kill her right here in front of you."

There was a wildness in his eyes that chilled Reed to the core. Will was a desperate man, and that also made him a dangerous one.

Emma swayed a bit. Blood dripped down her neck, disappearing into the collar of her shirt. It wasn't possible to tell how badly she'd been injured but it was enough to cause him serious concern. Reed met her gaze. With his eyes, he tried to say all the words he couldn't out loud.

I love you. Hold on. I'll get us out of this.

"We can put a stop to this now, Will. Things haven't gone too far yet. A man like you doesn't deserve to be in jail." It took every ounce of Reed's law enforcement training to keep his expression sympathetic, to have the lies fall from his lips without a hint of his true feelings. "Why don't you tell me what this is really about? We can fix it."

"It's too late for that now. Emma should've left when I told her to. None of this would've happened if she had."

Reed racked his brain, desperate to keep Will talking. "You were trying to prevent Bonnie's vehicle from being found."

"Duh." Will sneered. "I knew if Bonnie's car was uncovered, the investigation into her disappearance would be given a fresh look."

Reed desperately wanted to ask if his sister was alive but held back. Will was talking, but a move in the wrong direction could cause him to clam up. "When Emma wouldn't leave, you hired Charlie Young to kill her."

Will knew Charlie because he'd been the prosecutor on several of the man's criminal cases. Owen had mentioned someone high up was protecting them. It had to be Will.

"It was supposed to be a simple hit," Will said. "Instead, the idiot, along with his family, made a mess of everything."

Reed kept his gun locked on Will. If an opening presented itself, he wanted to be in a position to take it.

"When Bonnie's bracelet was found in Emma's shed, you changed tactics." Reed edged forward, making sure to time his movements to his words, so Will wouldn't notice. "You decided to frame Joshua for everything. You killed Mike Young and placed his body in Bonnie's truck."

Will tightened his hold on Emma. Her face paled even more and her mouth pinched with pain. The trip down the river must've injured her ribs. It took everything in Reed not to cross the distance between them and tackle Will. Where was his backup? They should've been here by now.

"Why Joshua?" Reed asked, although he already knew. The point was to keep Will talking.

Will glared at him. "Nice try, Sheriff. I'm not stupid enough to waste time explaining things to you."

"Come on. We both know I'm not getting out of this alive. You've got me in an impossible situation."

"Exactly, so put your gun down before I blow Emma's head off."

"Come on. You've had me spinning my wheels for

weeks. Bonnie was my sister. At least, tell me how you outsmarted me."

Reed's skin crawled. He hated complimenting Will, but they needed time. Where was Cooper? SWAT should be in position by now. He glanced at Emma's shirt, where the wire was hidden, and his stomach sank. Will was blocking the listening device with his arm. Maybe the team had no idea they were in trouble.

Will was quiet for a moment, before a smirk played across his lips. "I did outsmart you, didn't I?"

"You've pulled off the perfect crime. No one suspected you. So, again, why Joshua?"

"I needed a scapegoat and you already suspected Joshua. I knew it would be easy to frame him for Bonnie's murder. Besides, he had it coming. That idiot actually thought he was good enough for Bonnie. I should've gotten rid of him a long time ago."

Will didn't know Owen had come forward to provide an alibi for Joshua. No doubt, he would tie up that loose end if given the chance.

"How long has Dean Shadwick been involved?" Reed asked.

"Oh, he's been my eyes and ears for a long time. There were rumors he could be bought for the right price." Will chuckled. "Surprise, it's true."

Reed's hand tightened on the weapon. He was going to find Dean and put him behind bars. There was nothing worse than a law enforcement officer who broke his oath to protect and serve. "You weren't driving your vehicle at the time of Bonnie's disappearance. Dean was, wasn't he? You told him to run a red light so you'd get a ticket and have an alibi."

"I knew I'd be a suspect since Bonnie and I had dated."

"Aren't you forgetting something?" Reed inched forward

again. Time was running out. He was wearing a Kevlar vest. If he could convince Will to take a shot at him instead of Emma, they might have a chance. "Bonnie's car is going to be processed for forensic evidence. Removing all trace of DNA is difficult."

"I know." The smile turned hard, and his gaze went flat. "If you weren't such a Goody Two-shoes, I wouldn't have bothered worrying about it."

"I can't be bought," Reed said, as the final pieces of the puzzle snapped into place. "You knew I was a liability. I'd track down any piece of evidence, run down every lead, to find the truth. Kidnapping Lily and Vivian was your way of getting me alone."

"Don't be so prideful," Will said. "I needed to kill Emma, too."

Lily had to be close by. There was no other explanation. And based off the fact that Bonnie's bracelet was discovered in Emma's shed, chances were, if his sister was still alive, she was close, too.

"Time's up, Sheriff. Drop your weapon."

It was now or never. Reed said a quick prayer and leaned forward on the balls of his feet. "We can make a deal—"

"There are no deals," Will screamed. He jabbed the gun farther into Emma's skin. "Now drop your gun before I kill her."

A guttural growl came from the trees. Reed caught sight of a flash of brown as it leaped out of the woods and tackled Will. Emma went flying toward Reed and he caught her.

Sadie! The dog sank her teeth into Will's arm, and he screamed. The gun, held in his other hand, went off. A bullet flew wildly, whizzing past as Reed tugged Emma into the woods for safety. A flash of blue appeared in the distance.

Dean? Reed raised his weapon, but the gait of the other man set his mind at ease. It was Austin. Backup had finally arrived. Sadie had been with his cousin, but the dog must've broken away when she heard the screaming. She'd rushed ahead to protect her mistress.

Sadie gave a yelp.

"No!" Emma screamed. "Sadie!"

Reed spun in time to see the dog fall back. Will sprang to his feet. Reed fired his weapon, but the other man was a moving target. He darted into the trees.

"Austin, he's on the move. I'm going after him."

Reed dashed after Will. They needed the man alive. He was the only one who knew where Lily was.

TWENTY

Emma rushed to Sadie's side. The dog was already on her feet. There wasn't any blood. Chances were Will had hit her with the butt of the gun. Sadie whimpered slightly when Emma touched her shoulder, confirming her suspicions.

Relief was short-lived. No other law enforcement stormed the clearing. Austin had disappeared with Reed after Will. The chief deputy had been alone. Will's iron clasp around Emma's chest must've interfered with the listening device. When things went silent, Cooper and the rest of the team hadn't known what was going on. Austin probably came quietly to investigate.

"Cooper, if you can hear me, Will Norton is the killer. He's escaped. Reed and Austin are in pursuit."

She reached into her pocket and pulled out Lily's lamb. She let Sadie sniff it. "We need to find Lily, girl. I know we've only done this in training, but I'm relying on you."

The dog's brown eyes seemed to mirror Emma's own worry. Based off Will's actions, there was no guarantee he wouldn't hold Lily hostage. She needed to find her little girl and she needed to do it now. There was no time to wait.

She gave Sadie the command to find. The dog took off into the woods. Emma bolted after her. "Cooper, I'm in the woods. I'm following Sadie in the hopes that she's tracking Lily."

She prayed they could hear her. Running through the woods while SWAT was storming the area was a bad idea. She could be accidentally shot by friendly fire. Still, it was a risk she had to take.

Sadie stopped, taking a moment to lift her nose to the air. Then she altered course slightly, taking them farther into Judge Norton's property. Sweat dripped down Emma's back. Her head ached. The wound in her scalp started bleeding again. Still, she pressed forward.

When her dog picked up the pace, Emma did, as well. Tree branches smacked her face. Her feet—clad in the stupid flats—slid along the pine needles. She tripped, flying forward. Her hands instinctively went out to brace herself. She hit the ground with a bone-jarring force. She sucked in a breath. Glancing up, she found herself face-to-face with a set of empty eyes.

Deputy Dean Shadwick. Dead.

Emma recoiled. Her stomach heaved. The man had been shot several times and left to rot half-hidden under a bush. From the looks of it, he'd been murdered recently. Maybe only hours before.

Will was cleaning house. Eliminating any threats against him. Emma staggered to her feet. A fresh sense of urgency fueled her steps. She feared her instincts were right and Will would use Lily as leverage to save his own skin.

In the distance, Sadie barked. The dog had passed over Dean as if he didn't matter. Hopefully, that meant Sadie was only tracking Lily's scent.

Shots echoed in the woods. Emma's heart stopped. They hadn't been close, but there had been several. She sucked in a breath as a few more followed.

Were they from Reed? Or from the SWAT officers? Or was that Will shooting? He'd been out to kill Reed. He wasn't going to give up easily. The worst-case scenario played in her head like a horror movie on fast-forward. Emma said a quick and desperate prayer.

The forest was dead silent. She waited two more breaths. Then Sadie barked again. Emma ran toward the sound.

A break in the trees appeared. A rustic cabin sat among the towering pines. The windows were sealed with large boards. Heavy chains and locks kept them from being opened. Sadie sat next to the building and barked once more. When the dog spotted Emma, her tail thumped.

"Good girl, Sadie." She patted the dog's head before circling around the building, looking for a way inside. It didn't appear as if anyone had used this cabin for a long time. Some of the shingles were missing from the roof and the wood siding was rotting. Yet several cameras hung from the rafters.

She rounded the corner. The cabin had a broken front porch. The only door was closed off by a heavy wooden bar across the front. Emma swallowed. This didn't look like a simple attempt to keep people out of the cabin. No. These were the kind of measures taken to keep someone *in*.

She gripped the wooden bar across the door and shoved. It wouldn't budge. The thing had to weigh more than she did. The wood bit into the palms of her hands. Her muscles trembled. Still, it wouldn't move.

Sadie growled. Emma spun.

Will stood at the base of the porch. His arm was bleeding and scratches from running through the woods marred his face. His hair stood up on end. He looked wild and unhinged. Her gaze shot to the weapon pointed straight at her chest.

"It's no use, Emma. You can't move it. And no one's coming to save you. Reed's dead."

No! It couldn't be. A hot rush of tears stole the breath from Emma's lungs.

"Once I kill you, I can convince the rest of the police department Joshua was behind it all," Will continued, almost as if he was speaking to himself. "He'll shoot himself, of course. Leave a nice suicide note full of apologies. Everything will be fine."

Emma's gaze flickered around. There was nowhere to go. No place to hide. Will had her trapped against the cabin. Emma played the only card she had left. She lifted her shirt to reveal the listening device. "Cooper knows everything. You won't get away with it."

Will's eyes widened. He cursed. The hand holding the gun shook. For one moment, she thought he was going to back off. Then something in his eyes snapped. He raised the weapon and trained it on her. "Goodbye, Emma."

A shot rang out. Emma waited for the pain, but nothing happened. Will's mouth dropped open. Blood bloomed on his shirt. It spread like a rapidly growing flower. He glanced down at it, incredulous.

Someone stepped from the trees. Emma blinked, her heart not quite believing what her eyes were telling her.

It was Reed. He was limping, his shirt torn and bloody. But he was alive.

Will collapsed. His gun clattered against the rotten boards of the porch. Emma kicked it farther away.

Things happened in a blur. Reed quickly closed the distance between them and slapped handcuffs on Will. Austin appeared. He began rendering first aid. Once it was safe, Emma launched herself into Reed's arms. She started sobbing. "He told me you were dead."

"No, Em. Not a chance." Reed cupped her face in his hands, swiping away her tears with his thumbs. "He took a shot, but he missed."

She sucked in a gulp. "Reed, I think Lily might be inside the cabin. I can't lift the bar off the door."

"I'll help you."

As they moved toward the cabin, Will struggled against the handcuffs and cursed. Emma ignored him. She took one side of the wooden bar and Reed took the other. As one, they lifted it.

Emma reached for the door handle, but Reed pulled her back. "Let me go first. Just in case."

She nodded. He led with his weapon, pulling the door open. She heard his sharp intake of breath. Were they too late? Had Will already hurt Lily? Maybe he'd killed her immediately after the kidnapping because he had no intention of ever giving her back.

She darted around Reed and then drew up short.

The cabin was decorated like a small house. A kitchen with a small sink and a hot plate sat to her left. A sagging twin bed was pushed against the wall. In the center of the room was a large eye hook cemented into the floor. A heavy chain was linked to it. Emma followed the length of the tether across the room to the far side of the bed. A woman was hiding in the corner.

Emma inhaled. "Bonnie?"

"You…you're real?" Bonnie asked. Her gaze jumped from Emma to Reed and then back again, almost as if she couldn't trust her own vision.

Beside her, Reed trembled. "Yes, we're real. I've been looking for you, Bonnie. I've been searching for a long time."

Tears streamed down Bonnie's face. She struggled to her feet. Emma came closer to help her and discovered why Bonnie was having so much trouble. Her heart soared.

Nestled in Bonnie's arms, sleeping soundly, was Lily.

Emma cried out for joy. She took her little girl and hugged her close, showering kisses on the top of her head. Tears filled her eyes.

"Is this your daughter, Emma?" Bonnie asked.

"Yes, it is. Thank you, Bonnie. Thank you for keeping her safe."

A flurry of activity followed. Deputies and other law enforcement descended on the cabin. Bonnie was freed from her chains and Reed helped load her into an ambulance.

Emma tightened an emergency blanket around Lily before bending down to pet Sadie. The dog nudged the baby's leg. "She's okay, girl. You did a great job."

Lily appeared completely unharmed. She babbled and giggled, waving her hands.

"Excuse me, ma'am." A deputy approached her. "The ambulance is ready to take you and your daughter to the hospital now."

Emma held up a finger. "I need just a moment."

Reed came toward them. Emma met him halfway. Without a word, Reed hugged them. His touch was gentle, and Emma rested her head on his chest. His heartbeat, strong and sure, thumped a steady rhythm.

Reed pulled back. "Go in the ambulance, Emma. I'll take care of Sadie. I'll get to the vet and have her leg checked out."

"No, I can't. Not yet."

Lily reached for Reed and he lifted her into his arms. Seeing the two of them together only cemented Emma's feelings. The Lord had given her a second chance and she wasn't going to waste a moment longer on her fears.

Emma took a deep breath. "I love you, Reed."

He drew in a sharp breath and locked eyes with her. Lily patted his cheek with one plump hand.

"I know it's bad timing," she said. "Horrible timing, actually, but you nearly died today and all I could think about when Will had the gun pointed at you was that I loved you." A fresh wave of tears pricked her eyes. "I didn't think there was anything worse than losing someone I love, but there is. It's not sharing the love in the first place. It's not telling the truth about how I feel. So I'm saying it now. Before something else happens and I don't get another chance—"

Reed lifted his hand, cupping her face. "I love you, too, Emma."

Her heart stuttered. "You do?"

"Completely and utterly in love. With you and Lily." He glanced at the little girl in his arms before focusing back on Emma. "When you told me you were leaving town, I was devastated. But I didn't want to tell you because Lily's safety, along with yours, had to come first. And I don't want you to be scared every time I walk out the door. I'll quit my job as sheriff, if it'll make things easier for you."

"No. Please don't. It's a part of you." Reed was a good man. The very best kind of man. Someone who would put the needs of those he loved above his own. "I won't promise to not worry, but every time I do, I'll say a prayer. You reminded me at the car, when Lily was taken and I was terrified, that she was in the Lord's hands. And so are you. I need to rely on Him to see us through no matter what comes."

He searched her expression. "Are you sure?"

"More than sure." Emma stood on her tiptoes and

brushed Reed's lips with her own. The kiss was gentle and light but filled with promise. "I love you."

"I love you, too." Reed's lips tipped up in a smile. "I hope that means I can convince you to stick around town."

"I don't need convincing." She touched Lily's back and returned Reed's smile. "I asked the Lord to help me make a home for Lily. He answered my prayers. Heyworth is where we belong."

EPILOGUE

Six months later

Reed tightened the last screw on the swing set. He placed his weight on the ladder leading to the slide, checking to make sure it would hold up. The screen door slapped against the house. Sadie barked and raced across the yard. Reed grinned and patted her on the head. "What do you think, girl?"

"She thinks it's a new obstacle course for her," Emma called out. A smile lit up her beautiful face. Reed's breath hitched. They'd seen each other almost every day since Will's attack, and still she had the power to make his knees weak.

"Sadie won't be too disappointed when she finds out it's for Lily, will she?"

Emma laughed and handed him a glass of sweet iced tea. "No. Not now that I've finished the big one over at the training center. We tried it out yesterday and she loves it."

"I'm glad." Reed wrapped an arm around Emma's waist and drew her closer.

"We have an audience," Emma murmured.

Reed glanced over his shoulder. Vivian, Bonnie and Aunt Bessie were sitting on the front porch with Lily.

The women were laughing at a story Vivian was telling. "They're distracted."

Emma playfully smacked his chest. "Reed Atkinson. For shame."

He swept in for a light kiss before releasing her with a chuckle. Sadie nudged his leg and he patted her on the head again. "Yes, yes, I love you, too."

Bonnie's laughter carried across the distance between them. It brought a smile to Reed's face. His sister wasn't completely healed from the year she'd spent as Will's captive, but in the intervening months, she'd made huge strides. He thanked God every day for sparing her life and giving them a new start. "It's nice to see Bonnie so happy."

"It is. Family and prayer have seen her through." Emma winked. "I think Joshua has had something to do with it, too."

Joshua was found in Will's house, tied up and drugged. Will had intended to kill him after Reed and Emma were both dead. The thought sent a cold shiver down Reed's spine. "I'm glad the trial is over. Maybe now we can all have some peace."

Will had survived being shot, but he was never going to see the outside of a jail cell, something that brought comfort to them all. Most especially to Bonnie. When Will had found out Bonnie was going to marry Joshua, he'd kidnapped her. Taking Lily had been another layer to the plan. He'd had some sick delusions of them being a family together.

Emma rested her head against his chest. "Let's not ever be the target of a criminal again, okay?"

"Sounds like a good plan to me."

"Should I get Lily out here to try the swing set?" she asked.

"Yep. It's ready."

Reed took a long drink of his tea, relishing in the sweet refreshing taste, and watched Emma stroll back to the house. Sadie bounced at her side.

It'd taken some time to rebuild Jeb's house along with the canine training center, but he'd never seen Emma more happy. She loved her work. Already she was starting to train a new set of puppies. The first one would go to the Heyworth Sheriff's Department. Austin had agreed to be the handler.

Emma helped Lily toddle down the porch steps. Reed quickly drained his glass and set it on the ground. As he expected, Lily broke away from her mom. She raced toward him on chubby legs.

He bent down and swung her into his arms. She squealed with laughter. "Okay, kid, I'm not going to be your personal swing anymore. I've built you a new one."

Emma chuckled. "Now you know that's not going to work. She's going to keep you and use the swing set, too."

"Is that true, little girl?" Reed tickled Lily in the stomach. Her nose scrunched as she laughed.

Sadie ran up barking. Her tail wagged.

"Don't worry, Sadie. I didn't forget about you." Still carrying Lily, he reached into the treehouse attached to the swing set and pulled out a box of biscuits. "A lifetime supply, remember?"

The dog barked.

"You spoil her," Emma said.

"She saved our lives. I can't spoil her enough." Reed handed the box to Emma. "Here, open that up for me while I put Lily in the swing."

His hands trembled as he slid Lily's legs through the holes on the swing's seat. Sweat beaded on his forehead. From the porch, Bonnie and Vivian's voices mingled with the music playing on the radio.

Emma opened the box and frowned. "What is this? That's not supposed…"

Her voice trailed off as she pulled out a diamond ring. Her gaze darted to him. Reed gently took the box, spreading the remaining few cookies on the ground for Sadie, before setting it aside.

He took Emma's hands and bent down on one knee. She inhaled sharply.

"Emma Pierce, I love you. I can't imagine my life without you or Lily in it. Will you marry me?"

Tears flooded her eyes. "Yes, yes. A thousand times, yes."

Reed let out the breath he was holding. He slid the ring on her finger before gathering her in his arms and kissing her. His heart soared. When they broke apart, he swiped the tears from her cheeks.

She laughed. "I'm always crying on you."

"Well, these are happy tears, and that makes a difference. But you go ahead and cry on me whenever you want. I've got you." He couldn't prevent every hurt from coming Emma's way, but he intended to be there to shoulder the burden alongside her. Without a doubt, he knew Emma would do exactly the same for him. "We make a great team, Emma."

She kissed him again. "Yes, we do."

From the porch a holler went up. Bonnie, Vivian and Aunt Bessie were jumping for joy and hugging each other. Lily clapped at their exuberance. Reed laughed as the women rushed down the yard to congratulate the couple.

His heart had never been so full. God had blessed him. Blessed all of them.

And he was thankful.

* * * * *

Dear Reader,

Thank you so much for reading my first book with Love Inspired Suspense! Reed and Emma's story was exciting to write, and I hope you enjoyed it, as well. Second-chance romances are a favorite of mine. They're a reminder that the Lord's timing is sometimes not our own. Which, if you're like me, can be frustrating. But it's also reassuring. With patience and faith, God will provide exactly what we need at precisely the right moment.

I often take ideas for books from real-life heroes. An article about the National Disaster Search Dog Foundation caught my attention. This nonprofit organization rescues dogs from shelters, trains them in search and rescue, and then places them with fire departments and other first responders at no cost. Emma's desire to start a similar training program was inspired by this organization and its mission.

I adore hearing from readers. You can find me online at www.lynnshannon.com, on Facebook, @lynnshannonbooks, or on Twitter, @lynnswrites.

Blessings,
Lynn Shannon